ANGELS

IN THE

ARCHITECTURE

BY

PHILIP WATSON

ACKNOWLEDGMENTS

Special thanks to my daughter and son, Kathryn and Chris, and my wife Lynn for their assiduous proof-reading.

For Lynn

My wife, without whose continuous encouragement and support this book would not have been possible.

ALSO BY PHILIP WATSON

Soft in the Middle

A Kiss From a Strange Lady

TABLE OF CONTENTS

FOREWORD

The Scarborough Writers' Society meets at the Red Lea Hotel in Scarborough on alternate Tuesday evenings – new members are always welcome.

For those not writing anything already the chairman, Bob Jackman, provides three words/phrases at the end of each meeting to be incorporated into a short piece to be read out at the next meeting.

Having used 'Charlie Chaplin' 'A Drunken Judge' and 'Blue Blood' to create one such piece, the other members of the Society encouraged me to continue with the story. This I did, using the words provided by Bob at each meeting as the titles of the subsequent chapters.

The development of the story was therefore not entirely within my control. For instance the 'Black Widow' character who appears in Chapter 5 came completely out of the blue and changed the mood of the story entirely. Likewise the 'Torn Stockings' in Chapter 10 brought in another pivotal character who had a significant impact on the plot.

I have retained the words as the titles of the chapters for the readers' interest.

CHAPTER 1

A Drunken Judge/Charlie Chaplin/Blue Blood

Weaving his way through the groups of spectators gathering for the grand finale (the Charlie Chaplin look-a-like contest) the 'Reverend' James Stephenson paused to adjust his Panama hat and stood for a moment to survey the scene before him. They had been blessed all day with long periods of unbroken sunshine; what few clouds had formed had been helped on their way by a warm south-westerly. In fact it had been a perfect day all round for the Ayton-le-Dale summer fete. Even the slight hiccough during the dog disobedience contest – the 'Reverend's' own little joke – when Billy Wilson's mongrel had bitten the judge's ankle before attacking the other contestants, had only added to the character and atmosphere of the event. James smiled at the memory and resumed his search for that same judge, the right Honourable Sir Jeremy Fitzebberston, who was no doubt still to be found in the hospitality tent, imbibing a medicinal scotch or six whilst his injury was attended to by the event's co-organiser, and designated 'First Aider', Mrs Atkins.

As he headed in the direction of the raucous shouts coming from the hospitality tent, the Reverend Stephenson couldn't help but reflect, that since the judge of the Charlie Chaplin competition was also the Right Honourable Sir Jeremy, little Billy Wilson's chances of winning the last competition of the day were slim to none. Still, it had been a grand day - no doubt about that. Almost a thousand pounds raised by the good folk of Ayton-le-Dale for the church roof fund. They'd as good as reached the twenty thousand pounds target the vicar had set himself when he'd arrived in the parish just eighteen months ago. If he'd believed in Him, the reverend would have been tempted to quote Robert Browning, 'God's in His heaven - All's right with the world.'

Inside the hospitality tent the vicar's senses were assaulted by the heat, the smell of sweat and alcohol, and a cacophony of chatter and laughter. Once again the beer tent was the most popular part of the fete. He scanned the crowd looking for his missing judge, and his eye was caught by the sight of a figure dressed incongruously in an immaculate dark suit amongst the sea of T-shirts and shorts. For a moment he thought there was something familiar about the man, something he couldn't place. But before he could focus to get a better look he was distracted by a commotion in the opposite corner of the tent. Sir Jeremy was lunging from his seated position at Mrs. Atkins, as she hauled herself to her feet having finished tending to his wounds.

'Come here you beauty!' he roared.

Mrs. Atkins pushed the Right Dishonourable gentleman roughly back down on to his chair.

'Get away from me you brute. You're drunk!'

The vicar looked around again for the man in the suit but he'd disappeared and once more the vicar was diverted by his star man's unruly performance.

'No, I'm not. No, I'm not,' slurred Sir Jeremy. 'I'm simply intoxicated... intoxicated by your great beauty. You remind me of the old colliers, the sort my family owned a couple of hundred years ago to bring coal out of Newcastle...sturdy, capacious and flat bottomed.'

'Flat bottomed?' said an equally drunk man leaning against the bar, pint in hand, 'You could park a bicycle between those cheeks!'

'How dare you sir?' demanded Sir Jeremy as he struggled to his feet. 'You are speaking of the woman I love!'

'Shut up you silly old beggar, before my husband hears you; or your wife for that matter,' said Mrs Atkins shoving him back on to his chair once more. This time the chair toppled over and Sir Jeremy ended up flat on his back. Within seconds he was snoring contentedly.

'That's all we need – a drunken judge for a children's look-a-like competition,' said the Reverend as he looked down on the sleeping drunkard.

'Well, *you'll* have to do it,' said Mrs. Atkins assuming her duties as co-organizer of the fete. 'That's all there is to it. Just don't give the prize to that Rupert Fotherington lad. His mother's full of her own importance as it is. Anyone would think she'd got blue blood'

The vicar took only a moment to consider the situation before realizing that Mrs Atkins was right. It would ensure a smooth ending to proceedings and, apart from the service in church the following morning, this could be his last public act in the village before taking his leave. He could also now make sure little Billy Wilson received some reward for his dog's exemplary behaviour in biting Sir Jeremy's ankle.

That evening, the Reverend James Stephenson sat in his study sipping a glass of single malt and counting the takings from the fete. There was over nine hundred and fifty pounds, making a total of over nineteen thousand pounds since he'd arrived in the parish; near enough to his target. It was time to move on. He'd earned the money – yes *earned* it; putting up with the devoutly righteous people of Ayton-le-Dale, preaching inspiring sermons to them week after week, ministering to their spiritual needs, consoling them in their grief, going to see them when they were sick. Oh yes, he'd earned it all right. How his twin brother had ever made a career out of being a priest he could never understand. But then, there had never been such two unalike identical twins. They were, or at least had been, complete opposites. Brought up as the sons of a devout and conscientious parish priest and identical in appearance, one, James, had followed in his father's footsteps, the other, Peter, had rebelled and gone completely off the rails. Whilst James had ended up serving as a missionary in Africa, Peter had ended up serving a prison sentence for fraud.

The 'Reverend' raised his glass, and said 'Cheers bro! Thanks for nothing!' He took a large swig from the glass and then set it down on his desk and pushed it away.

Why did his thoughts always return to his brother when he'd had a drink? Once again he found himself remembering that last, fateful meeting with James, yet another attempt by the righteous James at a reconciliation with him, Peter, his prodigal brother. James had just returned from his posting as a missionary, whilst he, Peter, had just been released from prison. They'd met at Peter's flat, where James had immediately regaled Peter with details of his new appointment as vicar in the parish of St Mary's, Ayton-le-Dale. And Peter had felt pleased for him, proud of his twin. At least there was one good apple in the barrel.

Why had James had to spoil it by taking it upon himself to give Peter a sanctimonious lecture on this being his opportunity to turn away from his evil ways and start afresh on the path of righteousness?

How could he, Peter, be expected to take all that again?

The 'Reverend' stretched for his glass and refilled it, as he recollected how all of the old feelings and conflicts had surfaced and the usual arguments had ensued, with James blaming Peter's behaviour for the premature deaths of both of their parents. He saw himself ejecting James from his flat as the argument continued out on the landing, and he told James exactly where he could stick his 'holier than thou' attitude. He saw his hands shoving James away, and the look of horror on his brother's face as he felt himself toppling backwards at the top of the stairs. Once more he relived every cry from James as, tumbling to the bottom, he hit one stair after another. The 'Reverend' felt revulsion at the haste with which he'd seized his opportunity, and, without a moment of mourning for his twin brother, had taken advantage of the situation - the fact that they'd both been out of circulation for a number of years and still looked more or less identical. He felt more disgust as he remembered how he'd stripped his dead brother of his cassock and dog-collar and had swapped clothes with him. After that it had been a relatively simple thing to call the emergency services and report that he had called round to meet his long lost brother and found him dead at the bottom of the stairs. Peter Stephenson, convicted fraudster, had thus become The 'Reverend' James Stephenson, newly appointed vicar of Ayton-le-Dale.

Playing the part of a vicar had been no problem to Peter; he'd been brought up in a vicarage and heard his father's sermons week after week until he was old enough to leave home. Substituting his own cynical attributes with his twin's more pious attitudes had quickly earned him the respect and affection of his new parishioners. But, as he'd had to acknowledge to himself more and more often recently, it was 'doing his head in'.

His thoughts drifted back to the beer tent; to the figure in the dark suit. He tried to conjure up a clear picture of the man, but couldn't. His gut was telling him that the man had been looking for him. And his gut was usually right. It was definitely time to go – even before the excessively pious devotion of his flock got too much for him. If he were right about the stranger then he wasn't safe in Ayton-le-Dale any longer. And perhaps if he surrendered his dead brother's persona and was no longer walking in the dead man's shoes, he would not be haunted by the memories of his brother's' death. It was time to take the money and run; not a new strategy for him. One last sermon on the eighth commandment; 'Thou Shalt Not Steal' and he'd be gone.

But what about that stranger? If his gut was were right about him how long did he have? He needed to buy some time – a single day would do. He picked up his mobile phone and punched out a text message, 'Got your money. Will bring it to you on Monday 7pm... Stephenson'. That should do it.

He took another sip of single malt and listened. Was that thunder? Damn it. Yes, it was. It was raining. And that meant the roof had to leak. That's what all of the fund raising had been for since he'd arrived. That meant water would have to be dripping into the church, just to the left of the altar as usual, when his parishioners arrived for the Sunday morning service.

'Sod it,' he sighed as he walked to the kitchen to fill a bucket with water. 'Still, I can't risk anyone asking why the roof isn't leaking anymore. It's not as if I could tell them it was a miracle.'

He paused, bucket in hand as if considering the idea seriously before shaking his head. 'No, even this flock of sheep wouldn't be that stupid.'

He put on a waterproof jacket and walked, head down against the rain, from the vicarage and into the church. Taking care on the rickety wooden staircase that was far too dangerous for any of his aged parishioners to ascend ('Health and Safety and all that,' he'd told them) he climbed to the top of the church tower. There, he poured the contents of the bucket into an old barrel. He repeated the trip several times until the barrel was about three-quarters full. Then he opened the tap at the bottom of the barrel until it just started to drip. All he had to do now was to place the bucket at the side of the altar to catch the drips. He knew that the bucket would be just about overflowing when his congregation started to arrive. They'd almost fall over themselves in their haste to be the one that would empty the bucket and replace it. Such a devoted flock. Such a stupid flock! For eighteen months he'd had them convinced of a hole in the roof. A hole they'd never seen, because the stairs were too dangerous for anyone to go up. But they'd seen the leak, seen the drips, and replaced the buckets themselves. What more proof could there be?

As he walked carefully down the wooden staircase he chuckled and said out loud, 'Well, "St James", oh brother of mine, if there really were a god and you were "up there" with Him, you wouldn't be letting me get away with this would you?'

At that very moment a flash of lightning struck the weather vane on top of the church tower. The lights went out momentarily, a clap of thunder that sounded like an angry roar caused the startled counterfeit vicar to turn and look up. In the sudden darkness he missed his footing and fell head over heels, landing in a misshapen tangle of limbs at the foot of the stairs.

The thunderstorm ceased almost immediately, the clouds dispersed and moonbeams flooded through the stained glass window, lighting up his face and giving an unnatural sparkle to the dead man's staring eyes.

CHAPTER 2

Two Cups of Black Coffee/Forbidden Rule/Bank Book

Mrs Irene Johnston arrived at the vicarage at her usual time for a Sunday morning – half past nine. All she had to do today was to make the vicar his breakfast and wash up; not the two hours general cleaning that she did from Monday to Friday. She liked to make breakfast for him on a Sunday: it was something personal she could do for him, to thank him on behalf of his parishioners – he was so gentle and considerate to them all. Then she'd leave the vicar in peace to prepare himself spiritually, as he put it, for the service, and go over to the church and open up. When Mrs Taylor arrived at quarter past ten, they'd get the hymn books and prayer books out and put the hymn numbers up in the rack on the wall.

Mrs Johnston rang the doorbell and waited, but there was no answer. 'Never mind,' she thought. 'He's probably still in the bathroom.' She opened the door with the key she used to get in when he was away on one of his sabbaticals.

'Father Stephenson!' she called. 'It's only me!' suddenly adding, 'Mrs Johnston!' overcome by self-doubt that she might have sounded too familiar.

Still no reply.

Irene wandered into the kitchen to put the kettle on while she waited for the vicar to come downstairs. After five minutes, she went to the bottom of the stairs and called more loudly, but still got no response. Perhaps he was in his study, concentrating on his sermon. She wasn't supposed to disturb him when he was in there, but she had no choice if he were to have his breakfast before the service. She walked through to the study and was surprised to find the door ajar.

Irene hesitated outside and called the vicar again. No answer. Should she go in? It was a forbidden rule. She was not allowed in the study. It was his 'inner sanctum'; the one place he could allow himself some personal time, and not concern himself with everyone else's cares and woes.

But the door was open. She pushed at it tentatively, peering inside the room as the door slowly opened. She could not believe her eyes. There, on the table, was an open bottle of whisky with an almost empty glass next to it. She'd never known the vicar to drink anything stronger than camomile tea. But even more surprising were the piles of banknotes on the desk. She took half a step inside the room, but hesitated again. There was the rule: she was not allowed in there. She looked over her shoulder, as if expecting the vicar to be standing behind her with a reproachful look in his eyes. He wasn't.

Irene took another step towards the desk... and the money, then another and another, until she was standing by the desk staring down at the precisely bound fifty-pound notes. She looked over her shoulder again towards the door, then back at the money. She picked up a neatly wrapped bundle. How much was it? She quickly counted the notes. Twenty: there were twenty fifty-pound notes in each bundle that meant there were... 'Fifty times twenty is...fifty times two is a hundred...that's it, a hundred pounds in each. No, don't be stupid. It's times twenty, not two. Twenty is ten times two so there's ten times a hundred in each bundle that's....that's one thousand pounds in each bundle! Oh my word! How many bundles are there?'

She did a quick count.

'Nineteen. That's nineteen thousand pounds and then there's some more there. Another few hundred pounds. Goodness me!'

Her eyes alighted on a bank book on the desk. Irene picked it up and looked at the inside cover. Name of Account: 'St Mary's Church: Ayton-le-Dale Roof Fund.' She turned the pages and saw the entries following the various fund raising events that the vicar had organised since he'd arrived. Irene smiled. He'd worked so hard.

But what was the money doing on the desk? She turned another page and saw a withdrawal closing the account. Why had the vicar taken the money out? They were less than half way to the total he said they needed. Had he found someone cheaper to fix the roof? Did he have to pay something in advance? Whatever it was, he shouldn't have left the money out on the desk like that, and with the door open as well! She'd have to find him. Perhaps he was in church. She closed the study door behind her and made sure the front door was locked, before making her way over to the church. On the way she couldn't help thinking about what she could do with nearly twenty-thousand pounds. Buy her husband Bill a new mobility scooter. Poor old devil could hardly get out of the house now. And visit her sister in Canada. Oh yes, she'd have to do that – not seen her for twenty years.

Mrs Johnston paused, patted her grey hair gently, and pulled at her dress to remove non-existent creases, before entering through the side door, which let her into the vestry. It wasn't locked, so the vicar *must* be in there. She didn't call his name, as she expected to find him deep in prayer and didn't want to disturb him. She opened the inter-connecting door into the church as quietly as she could and tiptoed across to the front of the altar.

A blood-curdling scream echoed around the cavernous church momentarily terrifying Irene, until she realised it was her scream. The cause was the sight in front of her.

There was the vicar, his legs and arms sticking out at all sorts of unnatural and grotesque angles, like a game of 'Pick-Up Sticks', his head nestling in a halo of blood. She sat down heavily on the step on which the congregation knelt to receive communion. Gasping for breath, her face was as white as the dead vicar's, although his lips were blue. She was sure he'd been dead for hours and would be cold to the touch but she was too frightened to touch him. He must have fallen down those stairs. He must have gone up to check on the roof when the rain started last night.

'I wonder if he'd had too much to drink,' thought Irene before admonishing herself for thinking ill of the dead – especially a vicar. What should she do? Ring 999! That was it. There was a phone in the vicar's study. She hurried back there, this time breaking the forbidden rule without thinking.

Her call was answered almost immediately, 'Which service do you require?'

But Irene didn't answer immediately. She was staring at over nineteen thousand pounds on the desk in front of her. Nineteen-thousand pounds that no one else knew was there! She struggled to answer the questions she was being asked, stumbling over her name, her address; no, they didn't want *her* address, they wanted to know where she was now. She was thinking mobility scooter, trip to Canada, the rest to charity. No: mobility scooter, trip to Canada, new car, the rest to charity. No: mobility scooter, trip to Canada, new car, new carpet for the lounge, the rest to charity. No: mobility scooter...

The call ended - an ambulance and the Police would be there in ten minutes. What was she going to do?

She could take the money!

She took a supermarket carrier bag out of her handbag and looked at it. She could put the money in that. No one would know it was missing. She would take the bankbook as well, just to make sure.

No, she couldn't. She was in the house of God!

But this was a sign from God. He'd let her find it. God had known she'd be the one to find the money, because *He* knew she made the vicar's breakfast every Sunday.

It *was* a sign. God wanted her to have the money. He knew she wouldn't waste it.

Irene's hand reached out towards the money and drew back, and then reached out again. She was about to withdraw it once more when, as if with a mind of its own, it grabbed a parcel of money and stuffed it into the plastic bag. The decision was made. Now she was picking up the money as fast as she could and cramming it into the carrier bag. She was breathing quickly and sweating profusely. Finally, she picked up the bank

16

book and put in it with the money. She looked over the desk – looking for any more money or any sign that suggested there had been money there. There was none. She looked at her watch; the Police and ambulance would be there in five minutes. She had to go now – take the money home, hide it. She took a step towards the door and was momentarily overcome with guilt. She turned back towards the desk but then turned again towards the door. Once again a voice inside her said, 'It's yours! Take it!' All doubts finally suppressed, she almost ran out of the vicarage slamming the door closed behind her.

*   *   *

Just round the corner, whilst Irene Johnston was vacillating about the money, Pauline Derbyshire was placing two cups of black coffee on the small, circular pine kitchen table and sitting down opposite her husband Mike.

'We have to talk about it Mike. We can't simply ignore the problem. We've got fifteen-thousand on the credit cards, a mortgage we can barely afford and they've cut my hours, and it looks like your job will disappear at any moment.'

Dressed in a black skin-tight t-shirt and matching knee length lycra cycling shorts, Mike Derbyshire stared at his coffee despondently, 'I only said my job *might* go. I'll probably be all right.'

'No, Mike. You said your job will *probably go*. It probably *won't* be all right! We have to do something!'

Mike picked up his cycling helmet and started fiddling with the straps. Pauline was right but he hadn't a clue what to do about it. He could see no way out. All he could do was stick his head in the sand and hope the problems went away. He should be out on his bike by now.

'Well I can't talk now. I have a long ride to do today. It's Sunday. That's what I do on Sundays.' He stood up. 'And I don't know why you made me that coffee. I've spent all morning getting myself properly hydrated. If I drink that I'll be stopping behind every ruddy tree I pass.'

As Mike put his helmet on and fastened the straps, his wife said, 'I don't know how much more I can take Mike. I'm just about at the end of my tether.'

Mike turned away, mumbled something Pauline didn't catch and then added, 'I'll see you later. We'll talk then.'

As he closed the kitchen door behind him Pauline screamed, 'Don't bet on it! I might not be here when you get back!'

'Promises, promises!' muttered Mike as he mounted his bike and rode off, looking forward to the solitude of his ride in the countryside.

*   *   *

Meanwhile, Irene Johnston was sitting in her clapped out Ford Fiesta outside the vicarage. The money was on the passenger seat in the plastic carrier bag. She took a deep breath, trying to calm herself enough to drive safely, and turned the ignition key. The engine turned over but failed to start. She tried again, with the same result. She could feel her heart fluttering like a flock of butterflies. The feeling reached her throat and her chest felt strangely tight. She placed her hand on her chest and took a deep breath.

'Don't panic,' she told herself. 'Wait a bit and then try again. You don't want to flood it, whatever that means.' Her husband Bill was always warning not to flood the engine by turning the key and pumping the accelerator too much.

She turned the key and the engine spluttered into life.

Irene breathed a huge sigh of relief. 'Right that's it. I'm definitely getting a new car – one that doesn't flood.' The car hopped down the drive as she struggled with the clutch control. Once out on to the main road her mind started racing. What should she say to Bill? What could she tell people to explain her new found wealth? She'd have to 'inherit' it from some distant long-lost relative. Yes, that was it. She smiled and relaxed. It must be God's will. He'd made sure *she'd* found the money and now He'd given her a way to explain it.

Lost in her thoughts, Irene had not noticed the cyclist ahead of her. Nor was Mike Derbyshire paying much attention to the road as he fiddled with his MP3 player which had just started to play 'Money's Too Tight to Mention' - not a song he could bare to listen to at the moment. He didn't see the huge rain-filled pothole until the last moment and he had to swerve sharply to avoid it, taking him right into the path of Irene's Fiesta. Startled out of her reverie, Irene yanked violently at the wheel and the car shot off the road, missing Mike but hitting a tree.

Mike screeched to a halt, leapt off his bike and ran to the crumpled vehicle. He pulled the driver's door open and examined Irene. He tried to find a pulse in her neck but couldn't. He tried her wrist. Yes, he could feel something. And her chest was moving slightly. She was breathing! She was alive! Thank God. He ran back to his bike, took his mobile phone out of his saddle bag, dialled 999 and gave the necessary details. Then he returned to the car to check on the driver. Only then did he notice the plastic carrier bag on the passenger seat. Not wanting to reach across the old lady, he went round to the other side, opened the door and took the bag out. He looked inside it. Then he looked at Irene. Then he looked inside the bag again. There must be thousands of pounds in there! What was an old lady doing with all that money on the passenger seat of her car on a Sunday morning? As his brain began to click into gear he thought, 'More to the point does anyone else know she has it?' This was too good an opportunity to miss. There was easily enough here to clear the credit card *and* leave enough to give him and Pauline some breathing space until they found better jobs. He noticed the supermarket name on the bag and thought, 'They're right. Every little helps.' And it was going to help him. He thought no more about it. Having checked that the old lady was still breathing, not bleeding from anywhere, he shoved the carrier bag into his saddlebag, leapt on to his bike and rode off.

CHAPTER 3

A Love Affair Long Remembered/A Long Night in Glasgow/Corpse

Dressed in jeans and a waterproof jacket, Detective Inspector Tony Barton, known as 'Dick' to his friends and 'Sir' to his subordinates, sauntered into St Mary's church. He saw Detective Constable Martin Ashworth, known as 'Ash' to *his* friends and 'Ashworth' to his superiors, (he had no subordinates) admiring the rear view of the female forensic pathologist as she walked down the aisle towards the Inspector and the way out. The DI watched as she approached and ran his hand through his thick prematurely (in his opinion) grey hair and pulled in his stomach, as he always did when he saw her. He didn't know why; he was very happily married and old enough to be the woman's father.

As the pathologist passed she said, 'Morning sir. Wasn't expecting you. Your DC has my observations. Looks like an accident. I'll have a full report for you in the morning.'

'Thanks Jill.' She was obviously in a hurry so the Inspector said nothing more. Instead he joined DC Ashworth in admiring her rear as she headed for the exit. Without turning, the pathologist waved her left hand and called, 'Looking trim, Inspector!'

DI Barton allowed himself a congratulatory smirk. He was looking trim. Then he suddenly wondered if she had seen him draw in his stomach. Was she taking the proverbial? Hoping his blushing would subside before he reached the constable, he resumed his sauntering up the aisle, making a show of appearing relaxed, looking around, admiring the Norman architecture and stained glass windows of the ancient church.

'Good morning Ashworth. Who's the corpse?'

'Morning Sir,' replied the Detective clearly surprised to see the DI in front of him. His voice carried a hint of nerves as he answered the question. 'The local vicar, the Reverend James Stephenson, according to that lady over there; Mrs Taylor.'

The Inspector turned, and saw a white haired lady with an almost equally white face, sitting on a front row pew sipping a cup of tea, being looked after by a young WPC.

'Did she find the body?'

'Yes... well no....'

'Which is it Detective?'

'Yes, she did find the body. But she wasn't the first to find it. That was a Mrs Johnston.' The Detective looked down at his notebook, before adding, 'A Mrs Irene Johnston.'

'And where's she?'

'That's just it, Sir. We don't know. She reported the body from the phone in the vicarage but she's disappeared. So this lady, Mrs Taylor, found it again, when she came into the Church about fifteen minutes later. I've sent a PC round to Mrs Johnston's house. I thought she might have been in shock and gone home without really knowing what she was doing.'

'Good idea Ashworth,' replied the Inspector.

The Detective smiled at the rare bit of praise and relaxed - venturing a comment of his own. 'I didn't think you were around this weekend sir. I thought you were in...'

'Scotland? I was, and a right waste of time that was. Turned out it was not our man they had after all. It was just some small-time local scumbag. By the time I found out it was too late to get back down here, so I had to spend a long night in Glasgow. A bloody long night.'

'I expect they're all long nights in Glasgow.'

'You may well be right Detective, but don't let DCI Jackman hear you say that, or you'll be back on traffic duty. Born and bred in Glasgie he was, and he won't hear a bad word said about the place. Anyway, I was just enjoying a pleasant stroll with the dog to pick up a newspaper, when I saw the police car outside, so I thought I'd pop in. I've left the dog outside – don't let me forget him.'

The Inspector paused and looked down at the body, still a tangled mass of limbs. 'Time of death?'

'The Doc says sometime last night; probably between ten and twelve. Looks like he fell down those stairs and broke his neck - not to mention both arms and legs. Doc said it's unusual to get so many bones broken just falling down stairs.'

'Yes, I suppose it is. Anyone would think he'd upset his boss or something.'

Ashworth wisely smiled at his superior's joke. 'What I don't understand is, what he was doing going up those stairs at that time of night. They don't look particularly safe at the best of times, never mind in the middle of the night in a thunderstorm.'

'Checking on the roof I expect,' replied the Inspector.

'Sir?'

'Did you not notice the fund raising "thermometer" on the wall outside? And a big sign saying "Save Our Roof". Looks like they're almost half way to their target. That, and the pool of water on the floor and the bucket over there suggest that the roof leaks. So perhaps he'd been up to check on it when the storm started last night'

'Of course Sir,' said the Detective, feeling like he'd just been given a very basic lesson in observation and deduction - one that he shouldn't have needed. He looked round; keen to make an observation of his own.

'The bucket, Sir.'

'What about the bucket Detective?'

'Well, what's it doing over there?'

'I would imagine the good Vicar dropped it as he fell.'

'But why was he carrying it? Why was he bringing it *down*stairs? Why had he taken up there in the first place? I mean, he already knew there was a leak right? Surely, all he had to do was put the bucket in position to catch the drips.'

'Good point Ashworth. Thinking like a detective. Perhaps you'd better go upstairs and take a look.'

'Me Sir?

'Your idea Detective; only right that you should be the one to investigate. You nip upstairs and take a gander, while I have a word with Mrs Taylor here, about the Vicar - and the roof.'

While DC Ashworth started on his ascent, holding on tightly to the rickety handrail, DI Barton sat down next to Mrs Taylor, introduced himself and dispatched the WPC to make them both a cup of tea.

*   *   *

Fifteen minutes after her husband Mike had left on his weekly bicycle ride, Pauline Derbyshire was still sitting at the kitchen table; her hands cupped around the now empty mug of coffee. She stared sightlessly at it.

They were in a right mess. She couldn't see a way out; at least not one that her conscience would allow her to take. It wasn't Mike's fault they were in such financial difficulties. They'd both spent the money, both run up the debts. And it wasn't Mike's fault that his job was under threat at the exact time that her hours were being reduced. She couldn't leave him now; not when he needed her most. He'd stood by her when they'd found out that she couldn't have children, and then again when she said she wanted to go back to university in her late twenties. He'd been their sole breadwinner then. No, she couldn't leave now. Even though he was no longer the same man that had supported her all those years ago. Even though he was bitter and sullen; almost wallowing in the rut in which they found themselves, blaming everyone and everything for their problems. Even though the intimacy and magic had long since left their relationship. And even though she now had that same intimacy and magic with someone else – with Peter. She owed Mike. She would have to end her relationship with Peter. A tear ran down her cheek as thought about her life without him, without their stolen moments together. She remembered how it had started - fuelled by an almost unquenchable passion, as she sought escape from the misery and boredom of her marriage, and how it had developed into a totally fulfilling relationship, full of warmth and tenderness... and love. A true *love* affair. Pauline knew that there would be no others. It would be a love affair long remembered - never forgotten.

She slammed her hand down on the table. No! She wouldn't give him up. She couldn't. But she needed to do something, needed to take control. If she could just find a way to get them back on an even keel financially, so that she wouldn't be leaving Mike in such a mess then perhaps... But she knew that wouldn't happen.

Pauline sighed, stood up, rinsed out the mug and put it down on the draining board. She took her mobile phone out of her pocket and found Peter's number. She took a deep breath trying to find the right words, trying to find the courage...

The kitchen door burst open, and Mike rushed in clutching a plastic carrier bag, still wearing his cycle helmet and the biggest smile Pauline had ever seen on his face. Her phone slipped from her hand as she stood gawping at Mike.

'You'll never guess what's happened,' said Mike, dropping the bag on to the kitchen table and knocking the full cup of coffee he'd left behind earlier on to the floor.

'Bloody hell, Mike. Look what you've done. What on earth's the matter with you? What are you doing back so soon?'

'Never mind the coffee,' replied Mike, as it flowed slowly across the floor. 'Look in this bag. Look what I've found. The answer to our prayers!'

Pauline stepped cautiously over and peered inside the bag. There was the biggest pile of money she'd ever seen in her life. What on earth had Mike done? Robbed a bank? She could find no words. Instead Pauline stared at her husband in confusion.

'I know,' he said. 'It's crazy isn't it? I just found it... sort of.'

'What do you mean sort of?'

Mike replied, speaking almost too quickly to be understood. 'Well, this crazy old lady nearly knocked me off my bike and killed me, but she swerved and hit a tree. I stopped to make sure that she was all right, and saw this bag on the seat next to her.'

Pauline looked at Mike aghast. 'Don't tell me you robbed a dead woman!'

'No I didn't! How could you think such a thing? She was still alive!'

'What?'

'She was still alive. She was unconscious so I rang for an ambulance. Then I saw this money. And... well... I took it. I mean, I made sure she was all right before I left. She was breathing OK, and I couldn't see any bleeding. And, well, the money was just sitting there, and I got to thinking, "What's an old lady doing with all that money in a plastic bag in her car on a Sunday morning?" It didn't seem right. I thought perhaps she'd stolen it or something. Then I realised that no one knew I was there, and the old lady hadn't seen me properly, so I took it!'

Pauline dropped down on to a chair.

'You've stolen all that money.'

'Yes sort of. I prefer to think of it as *found*. Anyway I got off that road as soon as I could and rode back by a different route, so that if anyone saw me they wouldn't think I'd been anywhere near the accident.' He paused and smiled, as if awaiting congratulations for his quick thinking.

'Stolen,' whispered Pauline.

'Found,' insisted Mike. 'And there's thousands here. Easily enough to pay off the credit card. *And* have a holiday.'

'Thousands,' repeated Pauline. 'You've stolen thousands.'

'*Found!* Look I'm going to go and have a shower. Some pillock in a BMW splashed me on my way home. I'm sure it was deliberate. That'll give you time to digest our good fortune. Then we can discuss what we're going to do with it all. Perhaps at the Pub over some lunch. OK?'

'Yeah, whatever,' replied a still dazed Pauline.

Mike stooped to pick up Pauline's mobile and put it on the table in front of her, then he kissed her on the top of her head and went off for his shower.

Pauline looked at the phone. The screen still showed the name 'Petra' – her code name for Peter. It always made Mike laugh to think that she had a friend named after a 'Blue Peter' dog!

Mike had enough money to pay off the credit card now, and more. He wasn't in such dire straits. On the other hand he had just committed a major crime. But then he clearly wasn't prepared to look at it as such. This was her opportunity. Mike now had money. She didn't need to stay with him to help him through that problem anymore. And if she did stay, then she'd be dragged into being an accomplice to a crime. That was taking loyalty a step too far.

She made the call.

When Mike came down from his shower there was a note on the kitchen table:

'Dear Mike, I'm sorry but I have to go. I think we've both known for a long time that the spark between us has gone. Now you've "found" that money. You don't need my support anymore. Please use it wisely. Best wishes P.'

Mike gaped at the note for a while and then crumpled it up in his fist. 'Best wishes! Best wishes?' Fifteen years of marriage and all I get is a "best wishes"!'

He looked at the bag of cash on the table; the cash which, as he suddenly saw it, had just cost him his wife and marriage. He grabbed it and hurled it across the room. The bag split as it hit the wall spilling out its contents. Mike slumped into a chair and watched as the notes turned brown as they soaked up the coffee. Coffee that he'd spilled because he'd been so excited to tell her about *their* good fortune - about the money he'd stolen. Yes, she was right. He *had* stolen it; of course he had. But he'd stolen it for them... for her! And now she was gone. All he had was... How much did he have? He realised he still hadn't counted the money. He still didn't know how much he had. He smiled, and then oblivious to the coffee soaking into his trousers, he knelt on the floor and started to count.

CHAPTER 4

BBC/Strychnine/Chop Suey

DI Barton had extracted all the information he needed from Mrs Taylor about the fundraising activities the vicar had organised for the roof repair, and was moving on to ask her about her friend. 'Have you any idea why Mrs Johnston would have left after finding the vicar's body, without speaking to us? Is she shy or something?'

'Shy? Irene Johnston? I don't think so! She'd be on the BBC talking about it if she could. She loves passing on gossip – although it's *news* when she does it of course. She's not one to *gossip*. No, she'd have loved to have talked to you I'm sure. I can't think why she'd have gone off without waiting for you.' Mrs Taylor paused and then added, almost in a whisper, 'You don't think something could have happened to her do you?'

'I'm sure that's not the case. There'll be a simple explanation. We'll find her soo...'

'Sir!' A shout from DC Ashworth, as he reached the bottom of the church tower stairs, interrupted the Inspector.

'Excuse me Mrs Taylor; it seems I have an over-excited Detective Constable on my hands,' said the DI, as he stood and indicated to the WPC standing nearby to take his place. 'Yes Ashworth, what's so important that it requires you to interrupt my chat with Mrs Taylor?'

Ashworth waited until the DI reached him before replying in a low tone. 'There's no leak sir.'

'What do you mean, "No leak"?'

'There's no leak in the roof. There's just a big tank up there with water dripping out of a tap at the bottom. The leak's a fake!'

Inspector Barton took a moment to digest the new information before exclaiming, 'Well I'll be bug... blowed!' remembering just in time where he was. 'So if the leak's a fake, then the fundraising activities must have been a fake as well. The vicar must have been on the fiddle.'

'Unless it was Mrs Johnston.'

Again the DI paused to think. 'You mean Mrs Johnston, presumably with the help of someone younger and fitter, set up the scam and the vicar found out last night, so someone threw him down the stairs?'

'Yes sir.'

'Unlikely I think. But it would explain Mrs Johnston's sudden disappearance. Better find her Ashworth – as soon as. And we'd better start looking for the money. Mrs Taylor reckons it must be close to twenty "K".'

'Yes sir. I...' the DC paused. Now it was his turn to be interrupted, as loud footsteps on the stone floor distracted him. 'Ah, here's the PC I sent to Mrs Johnston's house. You found Mrs J, Constable?'

'Yes sir.'

'Well, where is she?'

'On her way to hospital. She'd crashed into a tree.'

'Oh great!' replied Ashworth. 'How bad is she?'

'I don't really know. She's unconscious. The paramedics think she might have had a heart attack.'

The DI took over. 'Thank you Constable. Right Ashworth, get someone over to the hospital to find out how she is, and be there when she wakes up. Meanwhile, you can start looking for the money. *You* can go and write up your report now Constable.'

'There's something else sir.'

The DI raised his eyebrows to indicate that the Constable should tell him what that something was.

'Well sir, the man that reported the accident – the one Mrs Johnston had. He's disappeared!'

'Disappeared?'

'Well, left the scene at least sir. And I thought with Mrs Johnston having left the scene here, that well, you'd like to know.'

'Damned right I do,' said the DI, looking up as if expecting some reaction to his language. Not getting one, he continued, 'What is it with the good people of Ayton-le-Dale? Are they all shy? Or are they all not so "good"? Did we get the person's name Constable or did they insist on being anonymous?'

'Oh, we've got his name sir. A Mr Mike Derbyshire. I got on to the station and we've got his address too.' He handed a piece of paper to the DI.

'Thank you Constable, good work. Right Ashworth, let's go and pay Mr Derbyshire a visit. Constable, you can forget about writing up your report for now. Stay here. No one goes in or out. We'll get someone out from the station to seal the place off as soon as they can.'

*   *   *

Unaware of his imminent visitors, Mike Derbyshire had finished counting his new found wealth and had put it in a holdall which, for the time being, he had stashed at the bottom of the wardrobe in his bedroom. He was now sitting in the lounge sipping a large whisky, while he tried to collect his thoughts, and plan what he was going to do next.

How do you deal with nearly twenty thousand pounds in cash without arousing suspicion? If he were to deposit it into his bank account, there'd be a clear trail if anyone came looking for it. Likewise, he had no way of paying off his credit card bill with it.

He could just blow it: go out and buy lots of thing he didn't really need, but that wouldn't be making sensible use of his good fortune. He could gamble it. If he placed enough bets then surely one would come up, and then he'd have come across the money legitimately. On the other hand, he'd probably lose the lot. He took another sip of whisky and suddenly it was obvious. He could simply *say* that he'd won it by gambling. That could explain it. He could split the money up and spread it across a few accounts, so that it wasn't such a large amount going into one account. No one, apart from Pauline, knew he'd been at the scene of the accident and his first instinct may have been correct; the old lady may have been up to something a bit dodgy herself. As far as he knew, no one else even knew she had the money with her.

The doorbell derailed his train of thought.

'Bollocks! Who's that?'

He got up and looked out of the window. There was a Ford Mondeo he didn't recognise parked outside, and two men standing at his front door – one in a crumpled brown suit, the other in jeans and a waterproof jacket over a checked shirt. They didn't look like JW's and salesmen didn't usually call on a Sunday morning. He supposed he'd better answer the door. So he did.

'Good morning sir,' said the one in the jeans. 'Mr Derbyshire?'

'Yes' came the guarded reply.

'I'm Detective Inspector Barton. This is Detective Constable Ashworth. May we come in?'

'Yes, I suppose so,' said Mike, stepping back to open the door fully.

The two detectives stepped inside. Mike's brain was racing. What on earth could they want? Did they know about the money? Were they here to arrest him? Should he confess straight away? He realised that they were looking at him, waiting to be invited further into the house. 'Oh sorry, you'd better come through.'

Mike led the way into the lounge and invited them both to sit down, which they both did. He took this as a good sign - at least they hadn't pinned him up against the wall and cuffed him. He thought he saw the Inspector glance at the glass of whisky on the coffee table in the centre of the room. 'Can I get you a drink? Tea or coffee I mean. I know it's a bit early for that,' said Mike, nodding at the whisky, 'but I've had a bit of a morning really.'

'So we've heard,' replied DC Ashworth.

'You have?'

Mike could feel himself sweating.

They knew.

'Yes, and we'd like to know why you left the scene.'

DI Barton gave DC Ashworth a reprimanding look. The young man had shown their hand much too soon. He realised it was his own fault; he should have made it clear in the car that he would do the talking.

'Left the scene?'

'Yes Mr Derbyshire,' said Barton. 'You reported an accident, but you weren't there when the emergency services arrived.'

Mike felt himself relax. They were here because he'd left the scene of the accident, nothing to do with the money, or at least that's what their questioning implied. And suddenly he'd thought of a perfectly reasonable explanation – one that would get him off the hook completely.

'Yes, I suppose I did. I'm sorry, but I had to.'

'Had to?'

'Yes, you see I was in the car with my wife.'

'Your wife?' interrupted DC Ashworth, receiving another hard look from his superior. He looked down submissively like a young lion put in its place by the head of the pride.

'Yes, my wife, Pauline.'

Ashworth resisted the temptation to ask where she was now, and Mike went on. 'As I said, we were out in the car, came round a corner and saw this car crashed into a tree. We both got out to help the driver, but she was unconscious. Then we realised that we'd both left our mobile phones at home, so I ran back to ring for an ambulance while my wife waited with the old lady.'

DC Ashworth looked up, about to ask another question but was silenced by a look from the leader of the pride.

'After I'd made the call I had a drink,' he looked towards the whisky, aware that he could be giving the impression that he was an alcoholic but he had another surprise for the policemen. 'And then I went back. I got there just after the ambulance had arrived, but my wife had already left.'

DC Ashworth fought every instinct in his body to ask a question and kept his head down.

'Your wife had left the scene?' said DI Barton.

'*That's what I was going to say!*' screamed a voice in Ashworth's head.

'Yes. I've not seen her since,' said Mike.

'Have you tried calling her?'

'Yes, she's not answering.'

'I thought you said you'd *both* forgotten your mobile phones,' interrupted Ashworth, unable to disguise how pleased he was with himself to have caught out Mr Derbyshire.

'I did. I'd forgotten, but then I remembered and realised that I couldn't hear it ringing inside the house, so she must have had hers with her after all.'

DC Ashworth looked at him doubtfully and Mike took this as the opportunity to complete his story and get himself off the hook. He looked down dejectedly before continuing, 'The truth is, I think Pauline's left me. We were having an argument – about money as usual - when we saw the old lady's car. She was saying that she'd had enough of me, and our debts, and that our marriage was over.' He paused, but neither of the policemen said anything so he went on. 'I presume she pretended that she didn't have her mobile with her, so that I'd have to come back here to make the call. She was pretty insistent that she'd be more use than me if the old lady regained consciousness. Come to think of it, she even suggested that there was no need for me to go back there. I suppose that was just a ploy, so that she could drive off as soon as the ambulance arrived.'

'Except that she didn't wait for the ambulance. She left before it arrived.'

Mike looked shocked. 'She left the old lady alone! God! She must have been desperate to get away before I came back. I'm sorry, that's terrible.'

'It's not your fault, Mr Derbyshire,' said Barton as he rose from his chair. 'You did everything you could. Have you any idea where your wife may be?'

'No, I'm afraid not.'

'Well, no doubt we'll find her soon enough. If you could just give the Constable the registration number of the car she's driving?'

Mike recited the number and the detective wrote it down, before commenting, 'And you say you were arguing about money?'

Mike smiled inwardly, so they did know about the money and now they'd be thinking that Pauline had it. *'Result!'*

'Yes,' he replied. 'Isn't it always money, or the lack of it, that causes the problems?'

'Thank you Mr Derbyshire,' said DI Barton extending his hand to Mike, 'No doubt we'll be in touch soon. We'll need a statement. You'll let us know if your wife gets in touch.' He handed Mike a card with his telephone number on it.

'Yes, of course,' replied Mike, as the two detectives stepped out through the front door. He watched as they walked towards their car. The DI seemed to be tearing a strip or two off the younger man but that didn't interest Mike. He went back into the lounge, picked up his whisky and sat down to congratulate himself. He had just diverted the police's attention to his wife. They believed that it was she who had left the scene of an accident and, if they really did know about the money, then they would clearly think that his wife had taken it.

'Brilliant!'

He downed his whisky and allowed his head to fall back against the back of the armchair. Closing his eyes, he let the scenario unfold in his mind's eye. DI Barton was arresting his wife, then he was interrogating her in a shabby grey interview room at the police station. She was telling her side of the story.

Mike sat bolt upright. *'She was telling her side of the story!'* She'd tell them the truth. How it had been *him* who'd taken the money and left the scene.

He needed to get to Pauline before the Police did. But how? And then what could he do? His mind was racing again.

He poured himself another large drink and took a swig. He'd invite her round for chat; tell her they could have a Chinese take away. She could never resist a 'Chinese'. Then they could work something out - come up with a story to cover each other.

And if he couldn't persuade her to do that - he laughed - he could always put strychnine in her Chop Suey!

CHAPTER 5

A Race/Father's Wish/Black Widow/Gambling Den

As Mike Derbyshire embarked on his race against the Police to contact his wife, a gleaming black Mercedes with dark tinted windows parked momentarily outside St Mary's church in the village before pulling away. Minutes later it was parked once more; this time in the Car Park associated with the village pub - 'The Black Swan', known locally as 'The Mucky Duck'.

The driver, wearing large black framed spectacles and dressed in a light grey Armani suit, white open-necked shirt and black shoes that were even more highly polished than the Mercedes, stepped out and opened the rear passenger door. He then moved around the door and offered his left hand. The offer was accepted by a slender hand with immaculately manicured red fingernails and a dazzling rock the size of Gibraltar adorning the middle finger. With an elegance rarely, if ever, seen before in the village of Ayton-le-Dale, Constance Tyler, also dressed in a pale grey Armani suit, which clung to her every curve, stepped out of the car and followed the driver into the Pub.

As they walked into the unusually busy lounge bar, every voice ceased and every head turned towards the door. Twenty-three and a half pairs of eyes stared at them, and complete silence reigned. As the man in the Armani suit made his way to the bar through the crowd, which parted for him like the Red Sea, twelve pairs of eyes – all of them women followed him. The other eleven and a half pairs – all of them belonging to men - followed the tall, slim, elegant, raven-haired woman, as she took a seat at the last remaining free table in the bay window. When she crossed her legs revealing more of her shapely thighs, Bob Marshall took out his glass eye and polished it before replacing it, as though that would give him a better view. At the bar, the man ordered a slim line tonic with ice and lemon and a single malt whisky.

'I'll bring them over,' said the landlord, feeling embarrassed by the behaviour of his regular customers. He didn't want them to scare off the strangers; they looked like they could afford to spend a bob or two in his Pub. The crowd parted once again, as the man made his way over to the lady sitting by the window.

As he sat down she said, 'Well John, we seem to have caused quite a stir.'

She uncrossed her legs and crossed them again the other way. Bob Marshall's glass eye steamed up with the excitement.

'We certainly do, boss,' replied John. 'They're obviously not used to strangers round here.'

'No, it may be a bit too late not to be noticed, but we'll make our enquiries as discretely as we can, and be on our way. And you'd better call me Connie in here. I've a feeling they might think we've come from another planet, if they hear you call me boss.'

The landlord appeared with the drinks and set the tonic water down in front of the lady and the single malt in front of the man. For his trouble, he received a stony look from the lady while the man swapped the drinks round.

'I'm driving,' explained the man.

The landlord's puzzled face cleared; totally oblivious to the fact that his overt sexism had just annoyed one of the most dangerous individuals in the north of England. Aware of the expectations of his regulars he asked, 'Are you just passing through, or visiting someone in the village?'

'Actually, we were hoping to take a look round the church. We've heard that it's so beautiful,' replied Constance. 'But there seems to have been some sort of commotion there. Do you know what's going on?'

The landlord's face lit up. 'Oh yes,' he enthused. 'The vicar was found dead in there this morning! Fell down some stairs in church and broke his neck.'

'Oh my goodness how awful!'

'And that's not all. The woman who found him, Mrs Johnston, had a crash on her way home and has been taken to hospital! Although goodness knows why she was driving home. She should have been waiting for the Police and Ambulance to arrive.'

'You mean she rang the Police but then left before they arrived?'

'Yeah! Stupid woman. They say she must have been in shock or something. Still a stupid thing to do. She obviously wasn't in any fit state to drive.'

Constance and John exchanged a look.

An idea galloped across the landlord's mind. 'Would you like to eat?'

'Yes, I think we would. Could we see a menu?' asked Constance with an engaging smile.

'No need,' replied the barman. 'It's Sunday today, so it's a roast: lamb, pork or beef.'

Constance smiled thinly. 'Ooh, we'll have to think about it. They all sound so tempting.'

Pleased with himself, the landlord returned to the bar to update his regulars.

'Right John, drink up, we're leaving,' said Constance, before finishing her whisky in one. 'Pity to rush it. That was not a bad little malt.'

As twenty-three and a half pairs of eyes watched them leave, the landlord called over, 'Do you not want anything to eat then?'

'No thanks,' replied the man. 'We're both vegans!'

'Bloody weirdoes,' muttered the landlord. 'What's a vegan anyway?'

'They were having you on,' said Bob Marshall. 'That's what Mr Spock was in "Star Trek". The one with the pointy ears. There's no such thing as vegans really. Mind you, I never got as far as looking at *her* ears.'

'Aye, she was better than a poke in the eye with a sharp stick. What do you reckon Bob?' shouted someone further down the bar.

'Sod off!' replied Bob, who'd lost his right eye when he was eight years old when he'd poked it with a sharp stick to find out what it felt like. No one had ever let him forget it.

Outside in the car, John sat in the driver's seat as Connie sat in the back reflecting on their encounter with the locals of Ayton-le-Dale. 'Did you notice how the barman addressed *you* the whole time? Never looked at me – even though it was me asking him the questions. He reminded me of my first husband. He was a stupid sexist pig as well. You never met him did you? Died of an overdose of weed killer – very careless.'

'Well, this isn't the cosmopolitan city of Leeds, Connie. People are a lot more old-fashioned in a place like this.'

'They can't hear us now – you can call me boss again.'

John grinned. 'Yes boss.'

Connie smiled. John was much more than an employee, and they had far more intimate names for each other when evening fell and the curtains were drawn. But he knew that.

'So what now Boss? It looks like that scumbag Stephenson has escaped our clutches. Find somewhere better for lunch and go home?'

'Oh, I don't think so, John. This is personal. You know why. Stephenson took me for a ride – took me for twenty grand. That was bad enough, but when he smiled at me and winked when we were there at his sentencing: as if he'd escaped me somehow…

'I remember,' said John. 'I remember thinking he had just signed his own death warrant.'

'So did everyone else who heard about it. You wouldn't believe how many offers I turned down to finish him while he was in Armley. People must have thought I was going soft. And I can't have that. We came here to get him and the money. *He's* gone, so now it's just the money. It's a matter of principle. Until I get my hands on it I'll feel like he *has* escaped. Stephenson said he had it and I believed him. The money's here somewhere, it must be.'

'Well we can't go looking round the church: not with the Police still swarming all over it.'

'That's true, but we could go and visit Mrs What's-her-name in hospital; the one who found him.'

'Mrs Johnston?'

'Yes, that's the one.'

'What about the Police?'

'What about them? Why should they be interested? They don't know that the vicar was a crook who owed *me* twenty grand. Whereas Mrs Johnston did a runner before they arrived. That doesn't feel right to me. And as my second husband always used to say before he fell into the Leeds-Liverpool canal, "you should always follow your gut instinct".'

'A lot of good it did him.'

'He did OK – until he fell into the canal. A lot better than my third husband; falling down all those steps by the Abbey at Whitby. I ask you!'

'Yeah, who'd have thought someone could fall all the way down one hundred and ninety-nine steps?' John paused before asking, 'Do you think you'll ever marry again?'

'With my reputation? Who's going to marry a woman known as the "Black Widow"?'

John raised his eyebrows.

'No, John. Why spoil what we've got?'

'Don't say I never asked.'

'*You* don't want to marry me. Look what happens to my husbands. Although no one can prove a thing.' The look in her eyes hardened as if daring John to make light of her comment. They both knew about the sometimes uncontrollable rages that took her over; and they both knew what those rages could make her capable of doing – *had* made her capable of doing. Then she looked uncertain and let her head fall back on to the headrest behind her. 'Do you think I've let my Dad down John?'

'How on earth do you work that one out?'

'Well, he always told me that it was every father's wish that his daughter should find a good man to marry and provide grandchildren.'

'Well, he couldn't say you haven't tried. You've been married three times and you're only thirty si...'

'Three,' Constance finished off. 'But I never married with the intention of having children. It was always for the money.'

'And what have you done with the money? You've taken a grubby little gambling den of your Dad's and built it into the biggest and most profitable chain of casinos and clubs in the north. *They're* his grandchildren.'

Constance smiled. John always knew the right thing to say. 'Come on,' she said. 'Let's find somewhere decent to eat. I'm starving, and then I have a web to weave.

CHAPTER 6

Wet Paint/A Horse/
Undertaker/Groped in the Dark

Mike cut across the car park of the Black Swan deep in thought.

He'd tried ringing Pauline but it had gone straight to voicemail, so he'd texted her, telling her that he needed to talk to her urgently.

Should he have told her the Police were looking for her? Would that have made her more likely to get in touch?

Either way, he knew she wouldn't go along with his stupid lie about her disappearing from the scene of the accident.

At the moment his only course of action – the only one that could keep him out of *serious* trouble - seemed to be to get the money back to the woman he'd stolen it from. Hopefully someone in the pub would be able to tell him who she was. That would still leave him with having to explain to the Police why he had left the scene and then lied to them about it. He hadn't a clue how seriously they'd view that behaviour. As he began to ponder the consequences of his stupidity; the probable appearance in court, being found guilty, the humiliation that would follow, possibly even losing his job, he was totally unaware of the large black limo heading towards him. A loud blast on the car's horn caused him to leap out of his skin. Totally disorientated, he froze momentarily like a rabbit in the headlights before leaping like a gazelle, far too late to make any difference, out of the way of the car which had lurched to stop inches from Mike's shins.

Having exhausted his animal impressions, Mike watched the driver's window open smoothly. He couldn't see inside as the sun was bouncing off the rear tinted window straight into his eyes. Neither could Mike quite make out what the driver said. He was only able to pick out several swear words which ended with the words 'need an undertaker'. As he watched the car move away, Mike regained enough of his composure to mutter 'Ruddy tourists,' before walking into the pub to try to discover the name of the old lady whom he had robbed.

'Hello stranger!' boomed the landlord's voice as Mike entered the bar. 'To what do we owe this honour?'

Mike tried to smile but it was more of a grimace. 'Just fancied a pint and some lunch.'

'No Pauline? Has she left you at last?'

'Why'd you say that?' demanded Mike sharply.

'Steady on Mike. I was only joking. A pint is it?' replied the landlord soothingly, sensing that he'd touched a nerve.

'Yeah, sorry. She's at her Mother's, so I have to fend for myself today. Thought I'd pop in for a pint and a bite to eat.'

'Not out on your usual bike ride then?'

'Yes. I mean no, not today. Whose is that car I passed on the way here? The one crashed into a tree. Any idea? Looked like a nasty accident.'

'Mrs Johnston. A bit strange really.'

Worried that the landlord was going to say something about the missing money and that the whole village knew about it, Mike nevertheless forced himself to ask the landlord to explain.

'Well, Mrs J finds the vicar's dead body in the church – he's fallen down the stairs that lead up the tower –so she rings for an ambulance, but then she does a *runner* before they arrive. And *then* she has an accident on the way home. God knows why she left the church. Shock I suppose. It can do funny things to people.'

'*You can say that again,*' thought Mike. He paid for his drink and took a sip while he gathered his thoughts. The vicar was dead and Mrs Johnston – *his* old lady - had found him but then left the scene. Why had she done that? He knew why *he* had left the scene. '*Blood and sand!*' he thought. '*Don't tell me she really had nicked the money as well!'* He had to talk to her – and soon. He took a longer pull on his pint.

'Is she all right?'

'I don't know. They've taken her to hospital,' replied the landlord.

'Right!' said Mike as he put his glass down on the bar, harder than he meant. 'I've got to go.'

'You've not finished your pint. And I thought you were having lunch,' called the landlord as Mike headed towards the door. But Mike was too focused on his problems to respond.

Outside in the car park Mike took stock of his situation. He had to get down to Scarborough General and talk to Mrs Johnston. There were risks with that. The police could be there, and if she had a husband no doubt he'd be with her. But he had to try. He realised that he was quite excited by it all and that surprised him. He was usually a very cautious individual. Then he remembered that he'd a few whiskies at home and then about half a pint of bitter in the Pub. It was Dutch courage he was feeling, and he should act before it wore off. He used his mobile to call for a taxi, and ten minutes later he was in the back of the cab on his way to the hospital and the doubts were starting to creep in. The last time he'd been filled with as much Dutch courage as this was at an office party about ten years ago. He'd been groped in the dark in a stationery storeroom by the department secretary, a married woman about fifteen years older than him. He'd reacted as any red-blooded twenty-five-year-old man would do, only to be interrupted by the woman's husband who'd seen them enter the storeroom together. It had very nearly cost him his job. As it was, he'd had to be taken to casualty to be checked over after the husband had finished with him.

Mike shuddered at the memory and resolved to be careful. But he had no choice. He had to talk to Mrs Johnston.

As he walked into the A & E department he was almost overcome by the smell of wet paint. Half of the area in front of him was curtained off with huge black plastic sheets hanging from ceiling to floor, hiding the painters and decorators working behind them. He could hear one or two singing along with the radio, until another told them to shut up and have a thought for the sick people on the other side of the curtain. Mike noticed a uniformed policeman standing by a coffee machine and he turned his face away from him as he made his way to reception.

'Hi. I've come to see a Mrs Johnston. She was in a car accident. She was brought in a couple of hours ago.'

The receptionist, a woman in her sixties, reading glasses hanging on a chain around her neck, looked at him suspiciously. 'And you are?'

'Erm...' Should he claim to be a relative? Would they let him see her if he wasn't?

'Are you a relative?' asked the receptionist bringing his internal debate to close.

'No, I'm the man who found her and rang for the ambulance. I just wondered how she was.'

The receptionist's face lit up with a huge smile. 'Oh that's nice! I wish there were more people who cared like you.' She looked around conspiratorially, 'Well, we're only supposed to allow relatives through, but I think I can make an exception for you. I'm sure Mrs Johnston will be pleased to see you. She's sure to want to thank you. You'll be pleased to know that she's going to be fine. They're just keeping her in for a while to do some tests. She's through that door on the right.'

Mike wondered what medical qualifications the receptionist had to be able to reassure him that Mrs Johnston was going to be fine, but he thanked her anyway, grateful for her belief in the milk of human kindness, and followed her directions.

He found Mrs Johnston sitting up in bed with her husband sitting in an armchair holding her hand.

'Hi, I'm Mike Derbyshire,' and to answer their puzzled looks he added, 'I'm the man who found you Mrs Johnston, and rang for the ambulance.'

Mr Johnston struggled to his feet and grasped Mike's hand and shook it vigorously.

'Thank you,' he said. 'Thank you so much.'
Tears welled up in his eyes. 'You saved her
life you know.'

'Oh, I just did what anyone would do.'

Mrs Johnston's surprisingly firm voice
interrupted the two men. 'I'm not so sure
about that,' she said, adding more softly to
her husband, 'Why don't you go to the
restaurant Bill? You've had no breakfast and
no lunch. I bet you could eat a horse by now.
It'll do you good to move around. You know
how you seize up if you sit for too long. I'll
have a nice chat with Mr Derbyshire and
thank him properly.'

'Well, I am starving. Are you sure Irene?'

'Of course I am. Mr Derbyshire will look
after me – he has done once already today.
Isn't that right Mr Derbyshire?' she said
giving Mike a knowing look.

'Of course. You go and get something eat
Mr Johnston. I'll stay with Mrs Johnston.'

'Well, if you're sure. And call me Bill. No
need for this Mr Johnston lark. And she's
Irene. I'll see you later then.' He kissed his
wife gently on the lips, made way for Mike to
take his place in the armchair next to the
bed and then picked up his walking stick
and shuffled away, leaving his wife and her
saviour alone together.

'Well, Mr Derbyshire; where is it?'

'It?'

'Don't play games with me young man.
You know very well. Where's my money?'

'*Your* money Irene? Are you sure it's yours?'

'What do you mean? Of course it is'

'I'll tell you what I mean,' replied Mike, gaining confidence from the look of apprehension in the old lady's eyes. 'I know that you found the vicar's dead body this morning, and that you left the scene before the ambulance arrived – just like I did. And I think you did that for the same reason I did – you found the money.'

Irene opened and closed her mouth and made some incoherent sounds, before Mike said, 'There's no use denying it Irene. It's written all over your face. I'm right, aren't I?'

Irene closed her eyes and nodded silently.

'So the question is,' said Mike. 'What are we going to do about it?'

Irene said nothing. She had no ideas of her own. A combination of the shock of finding the dead vicar, the car crash, and now this young man knowing all about her stealing the money had left her bereft of any capability of rational thought.

Mike could see that he was now in control of things so he spoke quickly and clearly. 'Right, here's what we'll do. We'll split the money between us 50:50.' Irene opened her mouth to protest but realised immediately that she was not in a negotiating position. 'We both need to explain to the Police why we left before the ambulances arrived. You can say that you were in shock – didn't know what to do and that you swerved to avoid a cat; that's why you crashed.'

'The bicycle! I swerved to avoid a bicycle! Was that you?'

'Yes it was, but that doesn't fit in with the story I'm going to give to the Police. You swerved to avoid a cat OK?'

Irene nodded.

'Good'

Mike and Irene spent the next twenty minutes talking about where the money had come from, with Mike expressing some doubts about why the vicar would have drawn it all out of the bank. Then they went over Irene's story again, finishing just as Bill arrived back from the hospital restaurant. Mike took his leave immediately. He was anxious to get in touch with the Police and correct his story. He just hoped they'd understand why he'd tried to blame his wife, and give him some credit for coming clean.

He stepped outside and took out his mobile and rang the number on the card DI Barton had given him. As he listened to the phone ringing he saw a familiar Ford Mondeo arriving in the car park, driven by DC Ashworth and with DI Barton in the passenger seat.

It looked like he was going to be trying out his new story on the Inspector a bit sooner that he'd anticipated.

CHAPTER 7

Colt 45/Darkness/She danced in seven veils.

DI Barton took his mobile phone out of his pocket just as it stopped ringing. The screen showed a mobile number he didn't recognise. He put the phone back in his pocket – if it were important they'd ring back again. As soon as DC Ashworth had parked the car, Barton stepped out and stretched his back as he looked around the car park. He saw Mike Derbyshire standing under the blue-roofed canopy above the main entrance to the hospital.

'Well I wonder what he's doing here,' said the Inspector.

'Visiting Mrs Johnston perhaps?' came the reply.

'Hmm...very possibly. But how does he know her name? Even you didn't give that away when we spoke to him earlier.'

Ashworth felt his hackles rise. The DI had already given him a right rollocking for telling Derbyshire too much too soon in their earlier interview, and he'd been hoping that that would have been the end of it.

'Well I won't say a word this time then.'

'No, you'd better not, and you can wipe that stroppy look off your face anyway. You're not a ruddy two-year-old.'

They walked in silence across to Mike.

'Mr Derbyshire. This is a surprise. Visiting someone?' said Barton.

'Er yes. As a matter of fact I was; Mrs Johnston - the lady in the car accident. I was just ringing you as well. I have something to tell you, but then I saw you arriving so I cancelled the call.

The mystery of the phone call solved, the Inspector asked, 'Mrs Johnston? Why were you visiting her?'

'To apologise. Look, can we go somewhere a bit more private?' asked Mike aware of the number of people who'd stepped outside for a smoke in front of the 'No Smoking on Grounds or Premises' signs pinned to the walls of the hospital.

'Of course. Let's go and sit in the car shall we?'

As they walked back to the police car, Mike walking between the two officers, DC Ashworth asked, 'So how did you find out Mrs Johnston's name and where she was?'

Barton shook his head and smiled at his constable's inability to keep his mouth shut but he let it go. It was a good question and put the pressure on Derbyshire without giving anything away.

'What? Oh, I asked in the pub. Nothing happens in the village without the landlord getting to know about it.'

They all got into the police car with DC Ashworth sitting in the driver's seat while the Inspector sat in the back alongside Mike.

'I think you were about to tell us why you were apologising to Mrs Johnston,' said the Inspector.

Mike hesitated before blurting out, 'It was me who left the scene of the accident. My wife wasn't even there.'

'So why did you say she was?' Barton asked.

'To get her into trouble. Look, I was in the car alone. Me and Pauline had had a blazing row and she'd threatened to leave me! I told her she could for all I cared and then I stormed out and drove off. When I found Mrs Johnston I rang for an ambulance, but while I was waiting I got to thinking about Pauline leaving me. I realized I didn't want her to and I had to get back to see her. When I got home she'd already packed. She just pointed to a note she'd left, picked up her car keys and told me to apologise to the taxi she'd ordered as she wouldn't need it now I'd brought the car back! When you arrived I was still angry with her and feeling sorry for myself. I knew I shouldn't have left the scene, so I said it had been her.' Mike paused before adding, 'I'm sorry. I expect you'll want to charge me for leaving the scene of an accident.'

'Probably not, since you weren't part of the accident, but you could still be in some trouble. Do you know where your wife has gone?'

'No, sorry Inspector. I suppose she may have gone back to Leeds.'

'Why Leeds?'

'That's where she's from – where I met her. She was dancing in "Seven Veils".'

Doing the "Dance of the Seven Veils?' jumped in the Constable.

'No,' replied Mike. 'She was dancing in a club called 'Seven Veils'. I was there on a stag do, so you can guess the sort of club it was. But even through the darkness I could see that she was drop dead gorgeous; a different class to the rest of the dancers. Anyway, *we* were all dressed as cowboys as the groom-to-be was called John James but we'd all called him "Jesse" at school. I paid for her to dance for me and when she finished she said, "Is that a gun in your pocket or are you just pleased to see me?" I said, "It's a colt 45 actually but that I *was* very pleased to see her". Then she took it off me and started to stroke the barrel. I didn't know where to look and then she got all self-conscious and we both burst out laughing. Turned out she was a student just trying to earn a bit cash to get her through Uni; not the sort of tart you usually get working in a lap dancing club. So we arranged to meet again and well... I'm sorry. You don't want my life story. I'm rambling. She's only been gone a couple of hours and I'm falling apart already.'

'That's quite all right Mr Derbyshire,' said DI Barton. 'You get off home now and try to relax. We'll get a full statement from you tomorrow. Let us know if your wife gets in touch. We'd still like to talk to her.'

'You would? Why? I told you, she wasn't involved.'

'Just routine,' replied the Inspector. 'Nothing to concern yourself about. Now if you don't mind, my Constable and I have to go and talk to Mrs Johnston.'

'Of course, sorry,' said Mike, before getting out of the car and heading off to call for a taxi. The sun was shining, the sky was bright blue and Mike felt that a huge weight had been lifted from his shoulders. He was feeling good. The Inspector seemed to have bought his story.

Noting the slight spring in Mike's step the DI turned to his Constable, 'What did you think of Derbyshire's story?'

'I felt a bit sorry for him, sir.'

'Did you? I thought he was about as convincing as Bobby Charlton's comb-over.'

'Whose, what?'

The Inspector tutted. 'Never mind Constable, let's go and see if Mrs Johnston can do any better. She still has a lot of explaining to do. And don't forget. *I'm* asking the questions.'

CHAPTER 8

A Medal/Blood on the Garden Gate/Four Aces

As he walked into A&E DI Barton sniffed at the air. 'You got a new aftershave on Constable?'

'Sorry sir?'

'Eau D'ulux with a hint of turpentine perhaps'

'Oh, ha, ha! Very funny sir!'

'Glad you agree. You go and have a word with that uniform over there chatting up the nurse. Give him a good rollocking for letting Derbyshire into see Mrs Johnston while I go and find her. Come and join me when you've finished wiping the floor with him.' The DI stepped over to the reception desk and held up his warrant card for inspection.

The receptionist examined Barton's I.D. and then his mode of attire. Obviously his casual dress held more sway with her and she was singularly unimpressed. 'Yes?' she said.

'Mrs Johnston, please' replied the Inspector, deciding that he could be just as taciturn.

'My! She *is* popular this morning. She's in cubicles through that door over there. You'd better check with a doctor first that it's OK to talk to her though. She'd had a nasty accident.'

'I will.'

The inspector made his way into the cubicles' area where he found Mrs Johnston sitting up on trolley reading a paperback, her husband sitting on a chair by her side reading a newspaper, and not a doctor nor a nurse in sight.

Mrs Johnston smiled when she saw she had another visitor. She was beginning to feel important, a feeling that was dispelled instantly by Barton's warrant card as the colour drained from her face.

She put her book down on her lap and stuttered, 'Yes, Inspector, how can I help you?'

Barton looked down at the book and read the title, 'Blood on the Garden Gate.'

'You like thrillers Mrs Johnston?'

'She certainly does,' interjected Mr Johnston. 'And the bloodier the better. Surprises everybody... a good church-going woman...'

'Be quiet will you Bill? The Inspector doesn't want to hear all about my taste in reading do you Inspector?'

'No, not really Mrs Johnston. I wondered if I could talk to you about your day so far. You've had quite a morning haven't you?'

'You could say that.'

'We bumped into Mike Derbyshire on our way in. He said he'd been to see you. What did he have to say for himself?'

'Mike? Oh, he came to apologise for leaving me in my car when I had my accident. You do know I had an accident don't you? Of course you do, otherwise you wouldn't be here.' She sounded as nervous as an oyster at low tide.

'Take your time Mrs Johnston. I'm not in any rush. You said Mr Derbyshire came to apologise. Did he say why he left you alone?'

Bill Johnston interrupted again. 'Something about worrying about his wife leaving him. Bloody rubbish. No excuse that. She left him anyway. I tell you, when he came in and said he was the one who rang for an ambulance I wanted to give him a medal. Then when Irene told me later about him leaving her in the car alone I wanted to go after him and belt him.'

'Bill, calm down will you?' said Mrs Johnston. 'I told you. There was no harm done. He was confused. Remember, I'd done the same thing myself earlier.'

'You mean when you left the vicar's body after you found it?' asked DC Ashworth, who had only just appeared at his Inspector's side and immediately received a furious glare from the DI.

'Yes, I'm sorry. I know I shouldn't have,' replied Irene. 'I don't know why I left. I was in shock I suppose. Can't really remember much about it.'

'Just tell us what you do remember Mrs Johnston,' said the Inspector.

'Well, I remember finding the vicar... in the church... just lying there...his legs and arms were all over the place. Horrible it was. Then I remember going back to the vicarage to phone for an ambulance. And then...and then I remember a cat...'

'A cat?' said the constable.

'Yes, there was a cat in the road in front of me... D'you know, I don't even remember getting into the car? Isn't that strange? Anyway, I swerved to avoid it and then the next thing I know I'm in here with a doctor asking me my name and if I know where I am.'

'And did you? Know where you were I mean?' asked DC Ashworth.

DI Barton, close to apoplexy, turned to his constable and growled a whisper in his ear. 'There's a vacancy just opened up outside as a "sleeping policeman". The job's yours with immediate effect. Get out.'

Ashworth opened his mouth to protest but thought better of it, and left.

'Sorry about that Mrs Johnston, an opportunity has just arisen that is too good for my constable to refuse. Could I ask you the same questions again, this time without the interruptions from my Constable – if you don't mind?' The Inspector looked at Mr Johnston to make it clear that he included the older gentlemen in his call for no interruptions. Bill Johnston gave out a slight 'Humph!' and picked up his newspaper.

'Right, Mrs Johnston, can we go back to when you found the vicar?'

Ten minutes later DI Barton found DC Ashworth standing outside the entrance to A&E.

'"Sleeping Policemen" are supposed to lie down in the road – not stand next to it.'

Ashworth held both hands up in apology. 'I know. I know sir. I fed her the answer about leaving the scene after she'd found the vicar's body. I'm sorry.'

'Yes you bloody did; so I had to go through it all again.'

'Did you find anything out?'

'Yes and no.'

'Sir?'

'She told me the same story as Mike Derbyshire; exactly the same story, using exactly the same words and intonations: "And then...and then I remember a cat..." and then the same words about not even remembering getting into the car. Exactly the same words, almost as if she'd practiced them, as if she'd been coached.'

The Inspector stuffed his hands into the pockets of his jacket and stared at the pavement for a moment or two. 'There's definitely something fishy going on here Ashworth. First we have a dead vicar, who may have been on the fiddle, and then we have two people leaving the scenes of accidents on the same morning; then Derbyshire turns up here, and when he thinks we've swallowed his story he walks off looking like he's just been dealt four aces; and you should have seen the look of on Mrs Johnston's face when I said everything was fine and hoped she'd be better soon. She looked as relieved as a turkey on Boxing Day.'

'So what do we do now sir?'

'You dig into our three subjects. Find out all you can about Mr Derbyshire, Mrs Johnston and the vicar – especially the vicar. It was his death that started the ball rolling this morning; find out where he came from, what he was doing before, known associates, what his parishioners thought of him, was he close to anyone in particular, all the usual stuff.'

'You make him sound like a villain, sir.'

'Do I? Yes, I suppose I do. Well, don't forget it looks like he was conning his parishioners out of a shed load of money for a non-existent leak in the roof.'

'I guess I'm half hoping it could have been someone else. I mean if you can't trust a vicar who can you trust?'

'A Policeman?'

'I wish.'

'Is that a confession Constable?'

'No sir. You're not a vicar, and even if you were I wouldn't trust you.'

'How quickly you've lost your faith.'

'What can I say? I've got cynical in my old age – I'll be thirty next month. Can I ask what you'll be doing sir, while I'm checking up on our dodgy vicar?'

'You certainly can Ashworth. I'll be at home. I only popped out for a paper! Come on you can drop me off.'

As Barton led the way back to the car at a brisk pace, the brightly shining sun lifted his mood and he smiled as he anticipated a 'Sunday Roast' with his wife and children. In the car, strapping on his seat belt, he sat back, closed his eyes and imagined taking the dog for a walk along the beach after dinner with the whole family, 'Hells Bells! Max! Ashworth! You let me forget the dog. He's still at the church. You'd better put your foot down.'

'Blue light sir?'

'Certainly. It'll be a matter of life and death if anything happens to that dog – mine!'

As Ashworth reversed the car out and drove quickly away, neither of them noticed the dark grey clouds gathering on the horizon, nor did they pay any attention to the large black Mercedes with dark tinted windows that took their place in the car park.

CHAPTER 9

Windmill/Naval Uniform/Bicycle

John Kilgallon stepped through the sliding doors into 'A&E' ahead of Constance Tyler – a habit he'd developed over the years to make sure it was safe for her. Constance stopped alongside him and looked around, getting her bearings.

'I like what they've done to the place, especially the plastic curtain. Shabby chic without the chic,' said Constance.

'Nice fragrance as well,' replied John. 'I just hope they haven't done *this* side of the curtain yet. My Nan's outside lavvy was in better nick than this.'

'Probably smelt better as well. I'm betting Mrs Johnston is behind those double doors next to that copper over there. You follow me in after you've dealt with him.'

Constance strode across the room, past the waiting patients, none of whom looked in need of emergency treatment and breezed through the doors before the policeman on guard could react. She heard John greeting the constable like a long lost friend as the doors swung closed behind her. There to her left was a lady she recognised; the one she was looking for.

'Irene!' she said. 'How are you? Feeling better I hope? My name's Deborah by the way. You can call me Debbie if you like.'

'Er... Yes, thank you. Are you another doctor?'

'No, not at all. But I do have a few questions for you.'

'Oh, are you from the papers?' asked Irene feeling a little excited at the prospect of some local celebrity.

'No, I'm not from the press. I've brought some things in for you. I thought you might like to have them at your side,' replied Constance delving into her large, black, Marc Jacobs handbag and removing a silver-plated photo frame.

She placed the black and white photograph on Irene's lap. Irene recognised it immediately. It was her wedding photograph. She was in the beautiful white wedding dress her mother had made for her. Bill was dressed in a smart naval uniform.

Bill began to rise to his feet, 'What the...?'

John arrived before Bill could finish his question and, holding out his hand, said 'Bill! Nice to meet you.' Bill held out his own hand in an automatic reaction. John took it and held it firmly, raising the index finger of his left hand to his lips to indicate that Bill should remain silent. Once again the colour drained from Irene's face, as her blood ran cold. 'You've been in our house. Who are you? What do you want? How did you find out where I lived?'

The questions gave away almost as much as her answers would. Constance smiled. 'The internet Irene. It's amazing. You can find out anything on the World Wide Web. For example, Nigel and I drove into Scarborough for some lunch today and saw a windmill sticking up in the middle of the town. I'd not expected that so I "googled" it on my phone and found out that there's been a windmill there for hundreds of years and that it's now a very smart B& B. In fact we might even stay there tonight if we don't get our business finished today.' She paused and turned to John. 'How's the policeman outside Nigel?'

Without releasing Bill hand John answered,' He'll be OK. I showed him that he could touch his wrist with his thumb.'

'Is it double-jointed then?'

'More dislocated really; he's gone to find a nurse,' replied John tightening his grip on Bill's hand causing him to gasp.

Constance smiled and turned back to an ashen-faced Mrs Johnston, who was looking from John to Constance and back again in a confused manner. 'No Irene, he's not joking. We wouldn't want some snotty-nosed copper listening in to our conversation would we? Now, where was I? Oh yes, the wonders of the internet. Of course it's a bit trickier to find someone's address but I've got a man, not much more than a boy really, who is an absolute wizard on the computer and can find anything on the World Wide Web. We call him "Spider" because he's so good on the web. Finding your address was as easy as pie to him.' She took out a second silver plated photo frame: this one with a colour photograph of two girls, both about eight years old, and placed it on Irene's lap. 'And you have such beautiful grandchildren,' she added.

There were tears in Bill's eyes, he looked about to cry out until John raised his finger to his lips again.

'Let him go please!' said Irene. 'I'll tell you whatever you want to know.'

Constance nodded towards John who released Bill's hand.

Bill dropped back into his chair holding his damaged hand protectively against his stomach. He looked at his wife, 'Tell them what? What can you possibly have to tell people like this?'

John raised his finger yet again to his lips and Bill fell silent.

'Now then Irene,' said Constance. 'You found your vicar's body this morning didn't you?'

Irene nodded.

'Then you rang for an ambulance but you left before it arrived didn't you?'

Irene nodded again.

'I'll let you into a little secret Irene. Your vicar was not all that he seemed. In fact he owed me money; a lot of money, and he was overdue with his repayment. I can't allow that sort of thing. It's not just about the money. It's the principle. I can't be seen to let people disrespect me. It's bad for business, so we had to find your vicar. One of my men found him yesterday at your summer fete, but he reckoned the vicar clocked him. So we came over today to catch him before he could do a runner. Unfortunately he died before we got to him. But I'm afraid I can't allow even death to be an escape. The vicar's debt has to be paid – in full. Like I said, it would be bad for business otherwise. Now *I* think that when you found the vicar you also found the money, and you took it, and that was why you left before the ambulance arrived. That much money can do funny things to people.'

'That's bloody rubbish!' said Bill. 'My Irene would never do something like that.'

Without looking at Bill, Constance raised her hand to silence him. 'Now then Irene, I am quite willing to believe that you were taking the money home for safe keeping or whatever other story you might come up with, but I need to know what happened to that money. I understand that you had an accident. Do you still have the money?'

Irene hesitated. Constance picked up one of the photographs and showed it to John. 'Have you seen what beautiful grandchildren Irene and Bill have?'

'Yes, it would be a pity if...'

'I haven't got the money anymore! Someone took it when I crashed,' blurted Irene.

'Who?' asked Constance.

'The man on the bicycle – I didn't see him till it was too late and I swerved and hit a tree. He took the money.'

'What's his name Irene?'

'I...I ...don't know.'

The Black Widow, her face now cold and hard looked at Irene with eyes as dark as a moonless night. 'Don't put your beautiful grandchildren at risk Irene. If I find out that you knew the man's name and didn't tell me...' She didn't need to finish the threat.

'Mike Derbyshire! His name's Mike Derbyshire.'

'Thank you Irene. Where does he live?'

'I don't know. Really! I don't know! Somewhere in Ayton –le-Dale. That's all I know.'

'OK, Irene, no problem,' Constance looked at John who took his mobile phone out of his pocket and dialled a speed-dial number.

'Hi Spider, it's me. Another name for you. Mike Derbyshire, lives in Ayton-le-Dale. Cheers.'

'Right Irene, we'll be leaving you now, but if you've not told the truth, we'll be back. OK? Anything else you want to tell me?'

Irene simply shook her head. John's mobile phone beeped and he opened it up and held up the screen to his boss. She smiled. 'See what I mean Irene, the wonders of the internet. Mr Derbyshire's address in less than a minute. Goodbye Irene...Bill'

Bill grunted. 'You'll excuse me if I don't shake hands.

John chuckled as he led the way out through the double doors checking that the uniformed constable had not returned. As soon as they were through the doors Irene whispered, 'Quick, Bill, give me my bag.'

'What? What d'you want that for?'

'Just give me it will you?'

Bill stretched forward and picked up Irene's handbag awkwardly with his left hand and handed it to his wife. She scrabbled around in it, pulling out a mobile phone and a scrap of paper.

'What's that?'

'Mike Derbyshire's phone number. I'll have to ring him and warn him.'

'You sure you should? You know what she said.'

Irene already had her glasses on and was punching in the number.

'I've got to Bill. I can't just let them find him. They might kill him!'

*   *   *

Mike Derbyshire was feeling quite pleased with himself, slumped in front of the television watching a re-run of 'Columbo', eating a doughnut. He had spoken to the Police and they'd swallowed his story; Irene Johnston had her story straight and should be able to deal with the Police, and best of all, the text he'd sent to his wife telling her that the Police were looking for her had got her attention and she'd rung him. He'd explained that he'd told the Police that she'd already left him when he got home and that she didn't even know about the money. He'd made it sound as though he'd lied to the Police for her sake. She'd been very grateful so she wasn't going to contradict him even if the Police did bother to track her down.

He was so relaxed that he jumped when his mobile phone rang. 'Guilty conscience' he smiled to himself as he took it out of his shirt pocket to answer it. 'Hello,'

'Mike? Is that you? This is Irene; Irene Johnston.'

The panic in her voice infected Mike instantly, like some deadly virus.

'Irene? What's the matter? Did you have a problem with the Police? You did stick to the story didn't you?'

'The Police? No, the Police were fine. Someone else had been to see me. A woman and a man. She said the vicar owed her money and they've come to collect it.'

'What's that got to do with us? You didn't tell them you'd taken the money did you?'

'She'd already guessed. And she forced me to tell her everything.'

'What? How?'

'The man dislocated that policeman's thumb – the one who was supposed to be guarding me and then he just about broke Bill's hand. They're really nasty Mike. Really nasty. They'd been in my house. They threatened my grandchildren Mike; that's why I had to give them your name.'

'What?'

'I had to Mike. I told you; she threatened my grandchildren, and she wasn't kidding.'

'Oh thanks a lot Irene.'

'I'm sorry Mike I had no choice. I want nothing more to do with it. You can keep all the money if you want, but if you take my advice, you'll give it to her when she gets there. Don't try and play silly buggers with them. They're dangerous.'

Irene ended the call abruptly as if emphasising that she was not involved anymore. Mike dropped his phone on to his lap and sat still for a moment. He was certain of only one thing. He didn't know what he was going to do. Suddenly the possibilities were charging around in his brain: give the money up; do a runner; go to the Police. He needed time to think - and he couldn't do it at home.

Ten minutes later he had thrown some clothes and toiletries on top of the money he'd already stashed in his holdall and was sitting in the back of a taxi heading towards Scarborough in search of sanctuary, a place to think and plan. Perhaps he'd try a B&B. Scarborough had plenty of them.

He'd heard the 'Windmill' was good.

CHAPTER 10

Two Bluebottles/Torn
Stockings/Mount Everest

Mike found that the last room at the 'Windmill' had been taken earlier that day, so he booked in at 'The Royal': it was close both to the centre of town and to the beach, and he wanted to take a walk by the sea – he needed to think.

He walked down through St Nicholas Gardens to the South Bay and turned left. As he strolled past amusement arcades, the clanging sound of the machines and the shouts of the Bingo callers washed over him, unheard. He continued on past the harbour up to the Luna Park Funfair, its old-fashioned big wheel revolving slowly like a clock. For once he was not tempted by the aromas emanating, normally so seductively, from the fish and chip shops and doughnut stalls: a sure sign that he was nervous...scared. He simply felt too sick to eat. He turned round, walked back to the beach front, sat down on a bench, and gazed unseeingly out to sea. From the lighthouse on the harbour wall across to the cliffs leading down to Filey and then south to Bempton cliffs, the sea was calm, almost still. The waves lapped gently on the sand as couples walked by the shoreline enjoying the last of the evening sunshine, now that the earlier thunderstorm had abated. Mike noticed none of this. Nor did he notice that the temperature had dropped, as he sat in the shade cast by the shops on the streets winding up the hill behind him. His stomach felt like Mary Berry was folding a cake mix down there, as his mind lurched from one thought to another, unable to settle and allow any logical or rational analysis of his predicament.

A wasp buzzing in his ear brought him back to the present. Only then did he realise he'd sat down on a bench next to one of the bins: crammed with fish and chip wrappers, fizzy drink cans and the general detritus of the many family days out at the beach, that had been enjoyed that weekend. He began to walk back to the hotel.

What the hell should he do? Still feeling too sick to think straight, he arrived at the bottom of St Nicholas Gardens, which led back up to his hotel. He looked up; tracing the way to the top. Mike knew that there were over a hundred and fifty steps to conquer as well as the short steep stretches of tarmac linking the steps. That was something he could do: he could run to the top. He'd done it before and he knew it would hurt. Probably more so today – after the drinking he'd been doing and the rubbish he'd been eating but the pain would at least banish the fear for a while.

Taking a deep breath he launched himself at the challenge. The first twenty or so steps were fine and then he started to breathe heavier. Half way up his legs began to ache, then his lungs began to burn and he was gasping for breath. He drove himself on, relishing the pain in his lungs and in his legs that was setting him free from his fear; pain that left no room for any other emotion. Eventually he staggered to the top. Gulping in huge lung-fulls of air and bending double, he almost crawled to a bench. A laughing voice called to him, 'You look like you've just run up Mount Everest.'

Mike dropped on to a bench, and looked at the woman who was now standing before him. With a blonde 'beehive' teetering like the leaning tower of Pisa on her head, eye makeup that made Dusty Springfield's look subtle, lipstick that looked like it would glow in the dark, a skin tight t-shirt showing enough cleavage to park a bike in, a skirt that was no bigger than a belt, torn stockings (fish nets of course) and bright red heels that looked a couple of sizes too big and were high enough to give some women nose bleeds, she was not what Mike needed, and the look he gave her showed it.

'Don't get the wrong idea,' she said.' I'm going to a "Tarts and Vicars" do.'

Mike laughed. 'Which one are you going as?'

'At least you still have a sense of humour. But seriously are you all right? You look like death.'

'Yes thanks, I'll be fine in a couple of minutes. I just need to get my breath.' His voice was as dry as sandpaper and his voice cracked as he spoke.

'What the bloody hell do you want to go running up there for?'

'I wanted to take my mind off something.'

'Did it work?'

'It did until you asked me about it. Now it's all flooding back.'

'Sorry. If it's any consolation I've had a pretty crappy day as well.'

'Bet it's not as bad as mine.'

'Can you beat being dumped by your boyfriend when you're supposed to be on a romantic weekend, just before you're due to go out to a party?'

'Really?'

'Yes. I was going as a vicar and he was going as a tart. Then he suddenly decided that he didn't want to get dressed up as a woman. I told him he was being a wuss, and that *he'd* be better going as the vicar. He said that would be fine with him as that meant I could go as the tart, which was what I was anyway! That was when I hit him.'

'What with?'

'The bottle of wine we were supposed to be taking to the party.'

'Shit! Is he all right?'

'I expect so. He was still conscious, and I *did* ring for an ambulance before I left.'

'You didn't hang around for the ambulance to arrive?'

'No, I let him watch me get changed into this tart's outfit – since that's what he thought of me, and then I left. But as I said; he was still conscious.'

'Bloody Hell there must be something in the water today.'

'What d'you mean?'

'Well, you're the third person I've heard of today, who's rung for an ambulance and not waited around for it to come. And one of them was me.'

'You did it as well?'

'Yes, an old lady had a car accident and *I* rang for an ambulance, and left before it arrived.'

'Why? She didn't call *you* a tart as well did she?'

Mike laughed a hoarse laugh, 'It's complicated.'

'You need a drink, why don't you come over to my hotel and have a drink in the bar? I'm only staying over there in 'The Royal,' and I've just seen the ambulance leave with Simon in it.'

'Simon? He your boyfriend?'

'My "ex" boyfriend, yes. My name's Lisa by the way.'

Mike replied with his own name, holding out his hand and shaking hers. 'Pleased to meet you Lisa. And I will come to your hotel for a drink because it happens to be where I'm staying as well.'

Lisa beamed at him, 'Great! Then you can tell me all about your day. Convince me it's worse than mine.'

Mike ignored that invitation, instead asking, 'What about your party?'

'Oh, I'm not going to that! I couldn't face all the questions about where Simon was and then *all* the helpful suggestions that perhaps if I went to the hospital we could sort everything out...' Her voice petered out; she stared into space.

'Is that what you want to do? Go to the hospital? You can you know. I don't need looking after.'

'What? No! I was just thinking I've wasted the last two years of my life with that tosser! I should have hit him harder. Do you want me to help you up?'

'No I don't, you cheeky tart. I'm not infirm.'

'You will be if you call me a tart again. Don't forget I've got "previous".'

Mike laughed hoarsely again. 'Let's get that drink,' he said.

As they reached the entrance of the hotel, the doorman held up his gloved hand to prevent Lisa entering.

Realising what his problem was, she said, 'It's all right. You saw me leave twenty minutes ago. I was going to a "Tarts and Vicars" party.'

'Oh yes. What as?' replied the doorman.

'Bloody hell!' said Lisa. 'Have all the men in Scarborough got the same script writer?'

'It's true,' interjected Mike. 'She's a guest here – same as me.'

The doorman relented and stepped aside.

Once through the door Lisa said, 'Look, I'm going to go upstairs and get changed. If anyone else asks me what I was going as, I'll belt them. Do you want to wait for me in the bar? I won't be long.'

'Sure. What do you want to drink?'

'Oh! A white wine please. Thanks.'

Mike watched Lisa as she tottered off on her sky-scraper heels, managing only to get half way up the first flight of stairs before she stopped to take them off. Then he headed into the bar, ordered a white wine and a pint of lager and found a quiet seat in a corner to contemplate just how much he dare tell Lisa about his day.

*   *   *

Mike had no idea that at that very moment, having been delayed only a few seconds by his locked front door, Constance Tyler and her right hand man John Kilgallon, were standing in his lounge taking stock of what he'd left behind – a half eaten doughnut and a half drunk cup of coffee sat on the coffee table. Two bluebottles buzzed around the doughnut, periodically flying off to thud into the window before returning to the food.

'Looks like he left in a hurry,' said Constance. 'Irene must have got brave and warned him we were coming. You go and have a look round upstairs. I'll look round here.' John disappeared, leaving Constance to wander around the lounge picking up photographs and examining the post left on the coffee table.

John was back in the room in a couple of minutes. 'There's clothes all over the bed, wardrobe door's left open. He left in a hurry all right.'

'Seems he's married,' replied Constance, pointing at a wedding photograph on the wall. 'And her name's Pauline,' she added, holding up an envelope addressed to 'Mrs Pauline Derbyshire'. 'But my guess is that he was here on his own before he left. There's only one cup and one plate. Check the phone.'

John picked up the digital cordless phone and pressed a button a few times. 'Here it is,' he said reading from the display. 'Pauline 07485321007.'

'Good, put that in your phone. And Mike's as well. That'll be on there. We'll give *her* a ring later and arrange to meet her tomorrow morning first thing. If she knows anything about what her hubby's been up to, she'll be expecting a call from the police. And if she doesn't, then it'll be a nice surprise for her.'

'Why don't we just ring *him* and arrange to meet?'

'Because, he's already running from us, which means Irene probably told him what you're capable of. He's not likely to want to meet you. Whereas if we have his wife...'

'So why don't we pick her up now?'

'There's no rush. It's Sunday. The Police are not likely to want to talk to her about anything routine on a Sunday evening, and we'll have to make it sound routine so she doesn't run as well.'

'Fair enough,' replied John. 'So what now?'

'Now? Now we have a four poster bed waiting for us John.'

'Your wish is my command mistress.'

'I know it is John. That's why I booked a four poster bed.'

CHAPTER 11

Zulu/Wrestling Match/A Thousand Kisses

Silence had fallen temporarily in the Barton household but it was not all peace and harmony. Sensing the atmosphere, the children of the house had gone to their respective rooms. Tony Barton was sitting in his favourite armchair by the coal-effect gas fire, pretending to do the crossword in his Sunday paper. Mrs Barton, Elaine, - the name he would use should Barton ever want to talk to her again - was in the kitchen. The two of them were engaged in a mental wrestling match. They both felt they had the other pinned to the floor and were waiting for the submission – for the apology. And the Inspector was damned if he was going to be the one to crack. He wasn't going to apologise. He had nothing to apologise for. It wasn't his fault that he'd had to go to Glasgow on a wild goose chase and then got stuck there overnight on Friday. And it wasn't his fault that he didn't get back home until late on Saturday evening. OK, he may have been slightly at fault there but he couldn't really have refused the local Superintendent's invitation to attend the match at Celtic Park on Saturday afternoon – at least not without causing offense. And he'd been under strict orders from his own 'Super' not to do that. Nor was it his fault that he'd stumbled on the vicar's death when he went out for a paper earlier that morning: and once he had, what was he supposed to do? He could hardly leave Ashworth in charge. How was he to know it wouldn't be completely straight forward? And it definitely wasn't his fault that it had started raining as soon as they'd finished lunch, so they couldn't go down to the beach as planned.

No: he certainly had nothing to apologise for.

There was a slamming of cupboard doors coming from the kitchen. Plates and pans were being banged down on the worktops. Elaine was making the point that *she* was doing all the work. Tony patted his paper flat in retaliation.

Elaine Barton was fuming. If that husband of hers didn't apologise soon, his life wouldn't be worth living. She hadn't minded that he'd got stuck overnight in Glasgow. She knew that he hadn't done that on purpose – after all, who would? Nor had she minded when he'd rung her up at quarter to midnight as drunk as a skunk, having been royally entertained by the local police force. 'Shorry I won't be home darling,' he'd slurred. 'I love you darling. I mish you. Do *you* mish me?'

She'd assured him that she did.

'Grand bunch of ladsh they are up here. Wouldn't let me buy a drink all night. Shaid I was there gueshht. But I do mish you darling. Have I shaid that already?'

She'd told him that he had.

'Well I do. But I'll make it up to you tomorrow night. We'll get the kidsh in bed early and then we'll have an early night. And I'll shmother you with a thoushand kishesh. You'll like that won't you? A thoushand kishesh.'

Elaine had assured him that yes, she would like it. Eventually she'd got him off the phone. It had been late but she hadn't minded. He always became soppy when he was drunk, and he always thought of her. At least he'd never be tempted to stray. And once he'd suggested it, she'd been looking forward to an early night with her husband. A thousand kisses might be a few too many – but that would depend on where he was kissing her.

But then he hadn't arrived home until late, and he was suffering from a raging hangover. Been entertained at a bloody football match by some local senior officer or other and had had another skinful. Not in a fit state to do anything, never mind smother her in a thousand kisses. And then to cap it all he'd disappeared again today for hours; when he'd only gone out for a paper. So they'd had to postpone their walk on the beach until *after* lunch, and then it had rained and he'd fallen asleep in front of the 'tele' watching 'Zulu' for the hundredth time! Well, if he didn't apologise, he was going to pay dearly. All she had to do was decide how.

The phone on the wall interrupted her thoughts and she answered with an aggressive, 'Yes?'

'Oh, er, is that Mrs Barton? It's DC Ashworth here. Is Detective Insp..?'

Elaine Barton cut the caller short. 'Just hang on,' she said.

Opening the kitchen door, she yelled 'It's for you!'

'Who is it?'

'You're the bloody detective. Pick the phone up and you'll find out.'

DI Barton stirred himself from his comfortable armchair and crossed the room to do as his wife had suggested and pick up the phone, 'Barton,' he said curtly into the receiver.

'Oh, hello sir, Ashworth here. I just thought you'd like an update.'

Speaking unnecessarily loudly, Barton interrupted the constable. 'What? Really? Are you sure? Yes, you were right to ring me I'd better come right away.'

'Sorry sir. There's no need for that, I just thought I'd let you know...'

'I'll see you at the station in fifteen minutes Ashworth. Good work!' bellowed the Inspector.

Replacing the telephone receiver in the kitchen as quietly as possible Barton's wife could hear her husband calling, 'You'll never believe it darling. Something urgent has come up. I have to go in straight away. I *am* sorry. Ruined the bloody weekend haven't I? With all this work stuff.'

'Oh, it can't be helped,' Elaine replied breezily. 'I know criminals don't just break the law on weekdays. You get off darling. I can see to the kids.'

Astonished by his wife's understanding attitude, DI Barton gave her a swift peck on the cheek, picked up a jacket and dashed through the front door, before it dawned on her that he was leaving her alone yet again.

As soon as he was out of the house Elaine went to one of her husband's other jackets hanging by the door, put her hand in its inside pocket and pulled out a leather wallet.

'Sarah! Ben!' she called up the stairs. 'Your Daddy's had to go out again but he's *so* sorry that he's ruined our weekend that he said we can buy ourselves a present each, and it doesn't matter how much it costs! Come on down! Let's see what expensive delights "Mr Amazon" has to offer!'

Her husband was going to pay dearly all right, with the emphasis on 'dearly'.

DC Ashworth was typing away at his desk as DI Barton arrived at the station, as promised, fifteen minutes later.

'Well now, Detective Constable Ashworth, what was so important that you had to drag me away from the bosom of my family on a Sunday evening?'

The DC was nonplussed. 'No sir... I didn't... I mean...'

'Relax Ashworth. I was kidding. I needed to get out of the house, although the wife did seem to take this latest call-out surprisingly well. So what have you got?'

'I thought you might like to know; Mrs Johnston has come clean.'

'Don't tell me. She'd been having a mad, passionate affair with the vicar and murdered him when she found out he'd been two-timing her with the Bishop!'

'How did you know?'

Barton smiled; Ashworth was beginning to get his sense of humour. 'It was the way she looked longingly at *you* – I could tell she's a bit of a goer....So what have you really got?'

'Like I said, she's come clean. Admitted to taking some cash from the vicar's study and that Derbyshire then took it from her. And she says that she thinks he might now be in danger, from some thugs who are looking for the money.'

'Right,' replied the Inspector. 'You'd better give me the details.'

'Just finished writing it up Sir,' replied the DC pressing a key on his keyboard, causing the printer in the corner of the room to splutter into action. He walked over to the machine picked up his report and handed it to his superior. As Barton read through it, Ashworth explained how flustered and worried Mrs Johnston had sounded, and how her story had lurched backwards and forwards chronologically from one incomplete sentence to another. Eventually, Ashworth informed the Inspector, with an air of self-congratulations, he'd been able to decipher her story and tell it back to her to make sure he had it straight. Then he'd rung the Inspector and typed up his report.

'So, in a nutshell,' said Barton, 'Mrs J finds the vicar dead at the bottom of the stairs in the church, rings 999, then finds the money on his desk, succumbs to temptation and makes off with it. On the way home she swerves to avoid a cyclist – Derbyshire - and is knocked cold. Then *he* rings for an ambulance before falling prey to the same temptation and making off with the aforesaid money. Then he visits her in hospital and they agree to keep schtum and split the cash between them. Then after he's left, a couple of thugs turn up – one male, one female – and threaten grievous things to her grandchildren as well as just about breaking her husband's hand. So she tells them that Mike has the money and gives them his phone number. Then she rings Derbyshire to warn him. And only *then* does she think of ringing us, by which time no doubt, Mr Derbyshire has done a runner with twenty thousand pounds in his wallet and two violent criminals on his tail... that about sum it up?'

'Yes sir. Although I don't think he could get twenty grand in his wallet.'

'No; quite, Detective Constable. Description of the thugs?'

'Both dressed in smart grey suits – the woman's had a skirt rather than trousers. She had dark hair to just below her shoulders. He had short, Kilgallon hair, and wore glasses with a thick black frame. Called themselves Debbie and Nigel.'

'OK. You tried to get hold of Derbyshire?'

'Yes sir. Just goes to voice mail. I've left a message.'

'Tried Mrs Derbyshire?'

'No sir.'

'Right try her. He may have been in touch. Tell her to ring us straight away, if he does contact her.'

'Yes sir.'

'Did you get anywhere with looking into the vicar's background.'

'Ah! Yes I did sir.'

'And?'

Consulting his notes the DC replied, 'The Reverend James Stephenson arrived in Ayton-le-Dale about a year ago. Before that he'd been a missionary in Africa. This was his first parish in the UK. Easing him in gently, I suppose. He's the son of a vicar and here's the interesting bit. He has, or rather had, an identical twin brother; one Peter Stephenson – the black sheep of the family; known gambler and conman. Died just before The Rev arrived in Ayton-le-Dale.

Peter had done time for fraud – just come out as it happens. The Rev found the body. He'd gone round to tell his brother about his move to Ayton and found him dead. And get this: at the *bottom of the stairs* outside his flat in Leeds.'

'Seems falling down stairs runs in the family. Anything else?'

'Not yet sir. I'll keep digging.'

'Not tonight Ashworth,' said the Inspector looking at his watch. You've done enough today. Just try to get hold of Mrs Derbyshire before you go. Leave a message if she doesn't answer. I'll get our boys in blue keeping an eye out for Derbyshire tonight. You can't do any more.'

The Inspector turned to walk to his office and paused as if remembering something. Looking over his shoulder he said, 'Good work Ashworth. We might be able to make a half decent detective out of you yet.'

In his office Barton made a couple of phone calls and put the wheels in motion in the search for Mike Derbyshire, including a watch at airports and seaports. He also put in a call to an ex-colleague, now based at a station in Leeds, and left a message asking for anything he could find out about Peter Stephenson.

Then Barton put his jacket on and headed home. Elaine had seemed to be in a very good mood when he'd left, and he was sure he'd made some promise the other night involving a thousand kisses.

And he liked to keep his promises.

CHAPTER 12

A Cough/Laughing Chinaman/Cat with Two Heads

Martin Ashworth breezed into the office at precisely five past eight. Whistling almost soundlessly (and tunelessly) to himself, he was looking forward to working with his DI today - hoping to build on the rapport he felt they'd established the previous evening. The open plan office was already almost full with other detectives working on the more mundane cases of petty crime that normally filled *his* day. This time he was working on something more interesting, more complex, something that would finally improve his profile with his superior officers.

He wandered straight across to DI Barton's office and stood in the open doorway. 'Morning, Guv.'

'You're late!' growled Barton.

Ashworth looked at his watch. 'It's only...'

'I *know* what time it is. *I've* been in for an hour. Even that lot out there, working on the unfortunate transgressions of the delightful crack-head scumbags, who add so much rich diversity to our community, were in before you.'

'Sorry, sir. I...Is that something I can help you with?' asked Ashworth, trying to see what his Inspector had been writing without daring to move any closer to his desk.

The Inspector put his pen down firmly on the pad of paper in front of him and sat back. 'D'you know Ashworth? I read an interesting article in the paper yesterday. In fact I read *every* article in the paper yesterday whether it was interesting or not. But this one had a moral, which I feel is very pertinent.'

'Really, sir?' asked Ashworth, anxious to appear keen to learn.

'Yes. Apparently a cat with two heads was born in Oregon in the U.S last week. A "Janus" cat, named after the Roman god Janus who was two-faced. It's very rare but not unique. Unfortunately it died two days later, and do you know what the moral is, Ashworth?'

'No, sir.'

'Two heads are not necessarily better than one. Now bog off and don't come back until you've got hold of Mr or Mrs Derbyshire. We need to find *him* as soon as possible.'

'Yes, sir. I'll get straight on it.'

DC Ashworth hurried back to his desk leaving DI Barton to pick up his pen and resume his doodling. That devious wife of his had stitched him up good and proper. He'd gone home last night thinking about smothering her in a thousand kisses only to find that she'd hit *him* almost a thousand times in the wallet. Having bought the kids a 'smart' TV each for their bedrooms (which went against everything they'd always agreed about TV's in the kids' bedrooms) *and* booked a weekend at a ridiculously expensive hotel and spa for herself and her sister, she'd run up a bill of almost a thousand pounds. He looked at his doodling. Rather unimaginatively he'd drawn a cow with his wife's head on it. Rather more disturbingly the cow was walking towards an oblong building with a sign, written in blood, saying 'Abattoir' mounted above the door. Blood was dripping from the sign. He shuddered. What did *that* mean? Had he just unearthed some deep psychopathic tendencies? He tore the sheet of paper off the pad and tore it into as many pieces as he could before screwing them up and dropping them into the bin. He loved his wife and she loved him. But they were going through a rocky time and it wasn't all down to his job. What, he wondered, would happen if he cancelled the orders his wife had placed? Would his marriage survive it? Would his children ever forgive him? What would his wi...?

A cough from the direction of the doorway intruded on his contemplations; a cough that said, 'Excuse me. Sorry to disturb you. Please don't bite my head off. I have something to tell you.'

Barton ignored the cough's entreaties and bit the cougher's head off anyway.

'Well?' he snarled.

'Sorry, sir,' said DC Ashworth. 'Still no answer from Mr Derbyshire and *Mrs* was engaged for a long time but…'

'I do hope you're going to tell me you've got hold of somebody…'

'Yes, sir, Mrs Derbyshire.'

'And?'

'Well, it's a bit strange sir.'

'What is? Your inability to get to the point?'

'Sir? No, sir. Mrs Derbyshire. She said we'd already spoken to her and that we were on our way round to see her already.'

'We are, are we? So why do I feel as though I'm sitting at my desk talking to a moronic detective constable?'

'Well, I didn't mean it was you and me going to see her. I meant that she said the police are already on their way.'

'No kidding? Did she give you their names?'

'No, sir.'

'Did you ask?'

'No, sir.'

'For Christ's sake Ashworth!'

'Sorry, sir. I'll ring her back and ask.'

'No you won't! You'll ring her back and tell her to get out of the house, if it's not too late. Where is she by the way?' DI Barton was on his feet and putting on the creased jacket of his suit.

'At a Mr Adams' house. Boyfriend I suppose – if she's left her husband. Just off Scalby Road.'

'Right, come on. You can call her on the way. And see if we have any cars out there who can get there sooner.'

'Sorry sir. Why…?'

'Whoever rang her, it wasn't the Police was it? *We* are the bloody Police. You! Me! And this lot. Nobody else.' shouted Barton waving his hand at the seated detectives as he swept through the general office area. 'We know that there are a couple of heavy duty thugs looking for Derbyshire. Do I need to draw you a picture?'

As soon as the Detective Inspector and his detective had left the office, the remaining detectives pushed back as one from their desks and sighed. Their DI had gone off on one again, but at least they weren't in the firing line. They almost felt sorry for Ashworth. Almost but not quite.

*   *   *

John Kilgallon sat waiting patiently for the traffic lights to change from red. He turned towards Constance Tyler and asked, 'What if this Derbyshire woman doesn't know where her husband is?'

'We'll just have to hope for her sake that he doesn't want her to come to any harm.'

'Then what?'

'What do you mean "Then what"?'

'I mean that I presume *you* mean we'll take her and hold her until he brings us the money.'

'Exactly.'

'So *I* mean what happens after he's brought it? What do we do with them?' asked John.

Constance simply raised an eyebrow.

'Not "The Laughing Chinaman"?'

'He's the best disposal engineer we know.'

'The man's depraved, perverted. What he does to them first is sickening.'

'That's what makes him so good at disposal; he can't risk them being found. And they're not likely to be identifiable even if they are found.'

'But these two aren't villains. They're not competition. They've not done you any harm. They've just got caught in the middle.'

The traffic lights changed to green and the long gleaming black Mercedes turned smoothly off Scalby Road, as Constance replied, 'Mrs D perhaps, but Mr D stole the money from the old lady don't forget.'

'Even so he doesn't derserve...'

Constance Tyler spoke sharply. 'We have no choice John. So far this wig and those stupid glasses of yours coupled with the hundreds of witnesses we could come up with to say we were in Leeds all day yesterday would be enough to keep us out of trouble, but once we take this woman, that's it. She'd never forget us. She can't be allowed to talk.'

John Kilgallon pulled up outside the address Pauline Derbyshire had given them, and sighed. 'I suppose you're right. You usually are.'

Constance smiled. 'I *always* am,' she corrected.

There were two cars on the drive.

'Did you ask if she'd be alone?' asked Constance.

'No. She just said she was staying with a friend. Peter somebody.'

'Well, it looks like he may still be at home.'

'You mean we'll have to take him as well? Another one for the Chinaman?'

'Unless you can put him out before he gets a look at us" replied Constance. She liked John's more sensitive side – as long as it didn't mean he was going soft.

'OK, I'll give it a go.'

They stepped out of the car and walked up to the front door. John indicated to Constance that she should stand to one side. Then he rang the doorbell and stood to the right of the door himself with his back against the wall.

Moments later the door opened. John stood still. After a second, a man's head appeared and John swung his left fist round in a smooth ark delivering a sledgehammer blow to the man's nose. There was no cry from the man. He simply toppled backwards into the hall and fell like a tree to the floor.

John immediately stepped inside, followed by Constance.

They could hear Pauline Derbyshire speaking on the phone, sounding very confused. 'What? Who are they then? But it's too late! They're already here!'

John strode quickly into the lounge to find Pauline standing holding her mobile phone to her ear, with her mouth open, aghast. Before she could say anything else he had snatched the phone from her and ended the call.

'Sit!' he said.

Pauline sat.

'Stay there.'

Pauline stayed there as John left the room. In the hall he handed the car keys to Constance who went back out to the car while he dragged the man's limp body into the kitchen. Constance returned with a roll of duct tape and then watched as John used it to tape Peter's mouth closed and secure him to a chair.

'Good work John,' said Constance. 'You may have just saved his life.' Then they headed for the lounge together.

CHAPTER 13

A Bent Penny/Father's Book/Boots

DC Ashworth stared at his mobile phone as the call ended. He turned to his Inspector, whose attention was focussed on the road as he drove with blue lights flashing, as fast as he dared at that time of the morning. Scarborough traffic was never as bad as Leeds but there was still the 'school run' to contend with.

'They're already there sir!'

'Damn it! This could get very messy. You'd better call for back-up. I'll try to get us there in one piece without knocking one of these bloody yummy mummies off the road. Why can't kids get the bus to school or even walk? I had to! In all weathers!'

DC Ashworth decided not to reply and instead called for back-up as instructed. DI Barton concentrated on weaving his way around bollards and between the parting traffic as the drivers responded belatedly to the wailing siren and flashing lights of the otherwise unmarked police vehicle.

*   *   *

Pauline Derbyshire had sat exactly as John Kilgallon had instructed, but as soon as the immaculately dressed man and woman entered the room she was on her feet demanding answers. 'Who the hell are you? I know you're not the Police. I've just spoke to them. And what have you done to Peter?'

Her hands clenched and unclenched as he waited for a reply, her nails digging into the palms of her hands. She felt beads of perspiration popping out on her forehead.

Constance Tyler smiled and casually let her handbag fall on to the armchair behind which she was now standing. 'That's no way to greet your guests, I must say. You make me feel about as welcome as a bent penny in one of my casinos' slot machines. Unfortunately we have no time to explain, since, as you have just intimated you have already spoken to the Police, and they are no doubt hurtling to the rescue as we speak. We must leave immediately. Let me see, do we have everything? John; mobile phone?'

John held up Pauline's mobile in response.

'And your friend is safely ensconced in the kitchen. Right we'd better be on our way.'

'Where?' screamed Pauline. 'Where are you taking me?'

'Somewhere where we can talk in peace; without being disturbed by the cavalry that's currently charging towards this address.'

'But why? What do you want with me? I don't understand.'

'If that's true then all will be revealed shortly. Well, in an hour or so. As soon as we are safe. Now I really must insist.'

Constance Tyler looked at John, who stepped behind Pauline, grabbed both of her arms and marched her out of the house. Half way down the driveway Constance stopped dead. 'Damn it John,' she said, pulling at her black leather gloves as though trying to pull them further on. 'I've left my handbag in there. You put her in the car, and get in the back with her. I'll drive. I won't be a moment.' She turned on her heels and walked swiftly back into the house.

Two minutes later Constance was in the driver's seat, her handbag dropped heavily on the passenger seat beside her, and she was driving south on Scalby Road before joining the A64 and heading in the direction of Leeds - keeping strictly to the speed limits of course.

*   *   *

DI Barton and DC Ashworth arrived at Peter Adams' home, precisely one and a half minutes after Constance Tyler drove away, too late to witness her exemplary driving. The DI looked at the house with a sense of foreboding. It looked like every other house in the street – an ordinary 1970's semi-detached with a driveway leading to a detached garage, and a neatly-kept lawn. It looked like every other house on the outside. But what was going on inside? There were

111

two cars on the drive. One was the Derbyshires'; he recognised the number plate. The other, parked between the Derbyshires' and the garage, was presumably Peter Adams'. There were no other cars parked close to the house. They were too late. Whoever had been posing as the Police had already been and gone.

Barton feared the worst, and although he knew that time was of the essence, he still felt a certain reluctance to enter the house. Forcing himself to act, he threw open the car door and said, 'Come on Ashworth; let's just hope Pauline Derbyshire's all right. It looks like our Police imposters have already left.'

They jogged up the drive and Barton rang the doorbell, waiting only a couple of seconds before impatiently ringing it again. Peering through the living room window he could see nothing untoward – apart from the absence of Mrs Derbyshire.

'Try the door,' he instructed.

Ashworth tried the door handle and it responded.

'It's open sir!'

'Right! Let's get inside.'

Calling out the occupants' names as he crossed the threshold DI Barton, cautiously led the way. He stepped into the living room first and quickly scanned the room but still saw nothing out of place. Then he went towards the kitchen but stopped dead in the doorway at the sight of the body securely taped to a wooden chair; head slumped forward and slightly to one side, eyes staring blankly; his blood and brains splattered on the wall like a newly discovered 'Jackson Pollock'. Blood still seeped from a neat hole in his temple, trickling like crimson tears across his cheek over the now redundant duct tape covering his mouth, and dripping from his chin to form a slowly expanding red patch on an otherwise pure white shirt. Barton swore and turned towards his constable to order him not to enter the room. But Ashworth was already standing as still as a statue, the natural colour of his face draining away until even his lips were pale and being slowly replaced by a sickly, greenish hue. 'You'd better get outside,' instructed Barton, 'Don't want to contaminate the crime scene.'

Ashworth was gone before his Inspector had finished the sentence. The DI looked around the kitchen and slowly entered the room. Evidence of a light breakfast – two empty cereal bowls and two coffee mugs stood by the stainless steel sink, otherwise the kitchen was tidy; tidier than his own at home ever was. He'd get the Crime Scene boys in, but other than determining the type of gun used, he was sure they'd find nothing. This had been a professional. He could hear Ashworth emptying the contents of his stomach outside and waited until the retching ceased before venturing to check on his constable's well-being. Finding him still bent double over a fuchsia plant, which was now dripping with the remains of the detective's breakfast, as well as its natural dark pink blossom, Barton patted Ashworth on the back. 'Not a pretty sight eh Martin? You all right?'

Ashworth straightened up and wiped his mouth with a tissue.

'Better than that bloke in there. It'll take more than a few sticking plasters from Boots to fix him.'

Barton smiled at Ashworth's attempt at bravado and thought it would be a good idea if his detective had something to do, 'Well, if you're OK,' said the DI. 'You can get on to the Crime Scene team. We need them down here "tout de suite". I'll do a quick check upstairs, though I don't expect to find anything, and then I'll get on to Superintendent Redman. He's not going to like this – no doubt it'll be all my fault.' Then, as he was turning away he indicated two uniformed constables who were getting out of a police car that had just pulled up, and added, 'And tell those two to stay here and not let anyone inside until the Scene of Crime Officers have arrived.'

*   *   *

Totally unaware of the bloody mayhem that had occurred already that morning – mayhem that he had effectively set in motion by his actions of the previous day, Mike Derbyshire sat up in his bed at the Royal Hotel and looked at the young woman still asleep beside him. He couldn't help but smile. She had that effect on him. He'd told her everything last evening. And she'd listened. They'd had a few drinks and she'd made a plan. Today, she would accompany Mike to the Police Station acting as his solicitor. Lisa had not lied to him – he was in trouble all right. But trying to run would only make it worse. Either the Police or the two thugs who were now looking for him would find him eventually. Yet he didn't feel worried. Somehow Lisa made him feel as though everything would be all right. When it had come to saying goodnight she'd been about to leave the hotel rather than go back to her room in case her now ex-boyfriend returned; in fact she'd brought her hold-all down to the bar to avoid going back to the her room at all. And Mike, being a gentleman, had offered to share his bed with her. Lisa had said that it would be churlish to refuse such a gallant offer and they had spent a wonderful night together. Mike leant over and kissed her bare shoulder and then sat back up. She stirred, turned over, looked up at him and smiled. Then she propped herself up and kissed him on the lips.

'Morning you,' she said.

'Morning yourself,' Mike replied.

Lisa rested her head on Mike's chest and ran her fingers up and down his thigh underneath the sheets.

'You realise, in my Father's book, this makes me a tart?'

'What does?'

'Sleeping with you on a first date. He wouldn't approve of that.'

'I hadn't realised we were on a date,' said Mike.

Lisa stopped stroking Mike's thigh, lifted her head, looked into his eyes and said, 'No you're right. We weren't on a date at all. It was just a chance meeting.'

'So you're not a tart then,' smiled Mike. 'And you can carry on with stroking my leg with your Father's approval.'

'I'm not sure about that,' Lisa laughed, stretching up to kiss Mike on the lips once more. As he began to wrap his arm round her, his mobile phone rang. He turned to look at the screen. 'Bloody hell! It's Pauline!'

Lisa's body sagged in disappointment but she said, 'You'd better answer it. She needs to know you're going to the Police.'

Mike picked the phone up, 'Pauline?'

'No, Mr Derbyshire, I'm not Pauline,' replied a male voice, 'but I can put her on if you like.'

'Pauline, are you there?'

'Mike! Help...'

Pauline was cut-off and Mike heard her cry out in pain. 'I'm afraid Pauline can't say anymore at the moment,' said the male voice. 'And I don't want to sound overly dramatic, but if you want to see your wife again, keep your phone with you. Do NOT contact the Police. I'll be in touch again shortly with instructions. And I hope for yours, and your wife's sake, you still have *our* money. If you have, then everything will be OK. But if you haven't...'

The call ended.

CHAPTER 14

A Tape Measure/Royalties/Size Ten Boots

An ashen-faced Mike Derbyshire dropped his mobile phone on to the bed.

'They've got Pauline' he whispered.

'Who has? What are you talking about?' asked Lisa.

'I don't know who. Didn't give a name. Said he wants his money. He's going to ring back. Said I mustn't got to the Police.'

'But you *have* to tell the Police.'

'I can't! They'll probably kill her if I do! And me!'

'Mike, you have no choice. Think about it. If they really will kill her if you tell the Police, what do you think they'll do to her, and you, once you've given them the money?'

'He said everything would be OK. Once they've got their money back they've got no reason to hurt us.'

'I'm not convinced.'

'Look, he knows from Mrs Johnston that we didn't know the money was theirs. We're both just idiots who were tempted by a lot of easy money. They didn't harm her did they?'

'I'm still not convinced.' said Lisa.

'You don't have to be,' replied Mike. 'It's my problem.'

'It's my problem as well. We're friends aren't we? I thought a bit more than that after last night.'

Mike half smiled. 'Of course we are. God! How fast things change. I woke up this morning, looked at you and thought everything was going to be all right. Now, it's all gone pear-shaped again.'

'So go to the Police!' pleaded Lisa. 'They have expertise in this sort of thing. They'll know how to protect you and Pauline.'

'Really? In Scarborough? You think they get a lot of kidnappings by dangerous criminals in the "oldest seaside resort in the country"? Anyway it's too late to protect Pauline. They've already got her.'

Lisa threw herself back against the headboard. 'OK, I take the point. So what now?'

'You go to work. I wait for the phone call.'

'No, I'll wait with you,' said Lisa.

'No you won't. You're a solicitor for goodness sake. I can't let you get mixed up in this. Look, I'll ring you when I hear something and tell you what they want me to do, in case... well you know just in case.'

Lisa sighed and looked Mike in the eye. 'OK,' she said. 'You're the boss. Better get dressed, I suppose: you'll have to be ready to go when they call.'

They climbed out of bed, showered and dressed, in almost complete silence - neither of them wanting to give their worries any substance by saying them out loud. After checking out of the hotel, Lisa made once last fruitless attempt to persuade Mike to contact the Police. Then she kissed him softly on the lips and said, 'Don't forget to ring me and let me know what's happening when you hear from them.'

'I won't,' replied Mike, holding her tightly to him one last time.

Then they went their separate ways – she in one direction and Mike in the opposite to sit on a bench overlooking the South bay and wait for the phone call.

*   *   *

Barton started walking towards the car at the bottom of Peter Adams' drive, pulling out his mobile phone from inside his jacket on his way. The phone began to ring before he had chance to make his call.

'Barton!' he answered unintentionally sharply.

'Bloody Hell Dick! What's the matter with you? No milk left for your cereal this morning?'

"What? Who's…? Oh, sorry Bill. This case I rang you about has just blown up in my face.'

'How so?'

'Someone's just had his head blown off,' replied Barton. 'One of our law-abiding residents at that.'

'Bloody Nora! You got time to talk to me?'

DI Barton was settling himself back in the driver's seat of the car as he replied, 'If you've got something useful to tell me. My next job is to ring my "super" and tell him what's happened. And I'm not particularly looking forward to that. So what have you got?'

'Well, you asked me to find out all I could about one Peter Stephenson right? Well, he wasn't one of *our* law-abiding residents. He was a con-man and a gambler. Did time for fraud. You probably know all that. He came out of Armley about twelve months' ago, and died *tragically* a few days later. Fell down stairs. His body was found by his twin brother – a vicar.'

'Thanks Bill, but we do know all that. The vicar died on Saturday night – he fell down stairs as well.'

'Blimey! Perhaps they were brought up in a bungalow and never got very good with stairs,' suggested Bill.'

'Yeah, perhaps,' replied Barton. 'Well, thanks anyway Bill. I'll buy you a drink next time I'm in Leeds.'

'Cheers, but I haven't really got started yet. And now you've got a murder on your hands...'

'So what more have you got?' asked Barton.

'Well, until you told me about your murder I thought it was probably just a load of rubbish but now...'

'Come on Bill, spit it out!'

'OK, like I said, I thought it was rubbish, but I've been hearing rumours that Peter Stephenson has been seen in some of his old gambling haunts in Leeds – within the past year! Or at least someone who looks very much like him. Could have been his twin brother one bloke said. His hair was a bit shorter and neater, and he wore glasses, but apart from that, whoever it was, was a dead ringer for the dead man. Pardon the pun. We all thought nothing of it. Presumed it was someone who looked like him. But now *you're* asking about him.'

'Do we know what this "dead ringer" has been doing in Peter Stephenson's old gambling haunts?'

'Same as everyone else; losing money. But he hasn't got into any debt. Not like Peter. Just been operating in the smaller establishments - the "Las Vegas", "High Rollers": those sorts of places. Another reason for thinking it was just someone who looked like Stephenson. But there was something that one guy said. He swore this other bloke was using the same system as Peter Stephenson did on the roulette wheel.'

'Know him well then, did this informer of yours?'

'Yeah, well enough. My guy works in one of the casinos that Peter Stephenson used.

Apparently Peter ended up owing a lot of money. This lookalike is not headed down that route yet. And he hasn't been seen anywhere near... Oh shit!'

There was silence on the phone broken eventually by DI Barton.

'What is it Bill? What's the matter?'

'Sorry Dick, I should have realised sooner. It's just that I knew nothing about the murder until you told me two minutes ago.'

'Realised what?'

'I was about to say that he hasn't been seen anywhere near Tyler's Casino; run by Constance Tyler – the "Black Widow" – took the place over from her Dad when he died. Turned a grubby little back-street gambling den into the biggest and most successful chain of casinos across the north. Three dead husbands to her name and no serious competition left in her line of business. The other casinos in Leeds – the ones this look-a-like's been going to are not really competitors - not in her league.'

'So she's been unlucky with her husbands and is a very astute business woman?'

'Unlucky with one husband perhaps; the other two died very conveniently, though we could never prove anything. Same with her competition and anyone who crossed her.'

'What? All dead?'

'Or disappeared, or put out of business one way or another. And the thing is Dick. Rumour has it that Peter Stephenson owed

Ms. Tyler the best part of twenty grand before he was sent down.'

'This Tyler woman got long dark hair and a sidekick that wears glasses?'

'No. She's got very short red hair.'

'She doesn't sound like our woman then,' said Barton.

'One hell of a coincidence if she isn't.'

'Hang on Bill. I need time to think. I'll ring you back in ten.'

Barton dropped his phone on to the passenger seat and let his head fall against the headrest and closed his eyes. Ideas began to form in his head. Could it be that simple? His mobile was ringing again.

'Who is it now?' he sighed. 'Hello.'

'Barton? Superintendent Redman here. What's all this about a professional hit on my patch? It's all over the station. Get back here now. I want chapter and verse!'

'Yessir,' replied Barton. 'I'll be right there.'

He started the car up, wondering how it had got all round the station so quickly, and then looked back at the house to see his DC on his mobile phone.

'Bloody Ashworth. I'll kill him when I get hold of him,' he thought, but had to make do, for the time being, with winding down the window and shouting, 'Ashworth! Stop gossiping and get off that bloody phone and start doing a house to house before you get my size ten boots up your backside!'

Ashworth stammered a 'Yes sir,' as he watched his Inspector driving away and wondered what he'd done wrong now.

Fifteen minutes later DI Barton was sitting across from his Superintendent explaining what had happened in the last twenty-four hours, resulting in the murder of one of the town's law-abiding citizens.

The Superintendent waited patiently until Barton had finished and then said, 'So let me get this right. You think the vicar who died yesterday in Ayton-le-Dale wasn't a real vicar: that the real vicar died a year ago and the one in Ayton was his evil twin who did time for fraud and owed a lot of money to a Leeds gangster, who came to Ayton yesterday to find the fake vicar and extract what he owed her?'

'That's what it looks like at the moment sir. Although we have a mismatch on the description of the woman.'

'Mismatch?'

'Yes, our witness says the suspect has long dark hair. Bill Jackson's favourite for the accolade of Ayton-le-Dale's "most wanted" has short red hair.'

'So what do you think?'

'I agree with Bill. It's too much of a coincidence. She's probably wearing a wig.'

'Christ! So now we have gangsters in disguise!' said the Superintendent. 'You couldn't make it up could you? I think this is definitely one for my memoirs.'

'Can I have half the royalties then sir? It's my case after all.'

The Superintendent smiled grimly. 'Solve the case today Barton and you never know. What are the chances of that?'

'How long's a piece of string sir?'

'If I wanted to know that I'd give you a flaming tape measure. Now what are the chances of you solving this case quickly? What are you going to do next?'

'Obviously we'll have to set up a Major Incident Team sir.'

'Obviously,' interjected the Superintendent.

'And we need to find Mike Derbyshire before Constance Tyler does,' the Inspector continued. 'And we need to find Constance Tyler before she does any more damage.'

'Right get on with it. Take whatever resources you need. I'll get our press officer up here and brief her. This is bound to go public soon.'

'Yes sir,' replied Barton as he stood up to leave the office. He closed the Superintendent's door behind him and took a deep breath. 'First things first,' he thought. 'Let's get Ashworth back here. I've got a bone to pick with him.'

*   *   *

Mike Derbyshire sat on a bench at the top of St Nicholas Gardens, looking out over the bay towards the harbour and the lighthouse. From a clear blue sky the sun sparkled on the sea as it lapped gently on to the sand. It was a glorious day for a walk along the beach but Mike was once more totally oblivious to the attractions of Scarborough's South bay.

For the umpteenth time he checked his mobile to ensure that it had network coverage. For the umpteenth time he cursed himself for being such an idiot. For the umpteenth time he wondered if Lisa was right: should he go to the Police?

Then the phone rang.

CHAPTER 15

Scotland/A Red Pheasant/Theatre

Mike reached out his hand and watched it trembling for a moment, before picking up his phone, 'Hello,' he stammered.

'No need to be nervous Michael,' replied the bright and breezy male voice. 'If you do as you're told, everything will be fine. Now I want you to start driving towards Leeds. I'll give you further instructions when you're getting close.'

'I can't!'

'What do you mean you can't?' asked the voice – no longer bright and breezy.

'I haven't got a car,' Mike explained. 'Pauline took it. I suppose if you've got her, she can tell you where it is and I can go and get it. I have some spare keys in my pocket,' said Mike, doing his best to convince the voice that he was not just being awkward.

'I know where your car is,' said the voice flatly. 'And you can't go and get it.'

'Why not? What have you done with it?'

Mike didn't get a response to his question – the voice had ended the call.

'We have a slight problem, boss,' said John. 'Derbyshire says he doesn't have a car: says *she* took it.'

Constance looked in her rear view mirror. 'You and hubby only got one car between you?' she asked.

Pauline nodded, unable to speak as her mouth had been covered with duct tape.

Constance checked her speed and found that it had crept up to over seventy, so she eased off the accelerator. John watched his boss's face as she drove. He didn't like what he saw. Things were not going smoothly and she was angry. Someone always suffered when she was angry. Suddenly she put her left hand in her hair and pulled. It came off, revealing short red hair. She threw the wig on to the passenger seat. 'I won't be needing that anymore,' she said. 'And you might as well take off those ridiculous glasses.'

John said nothing. He took the glasses off, put them in his inside pocket, and looked across at Pauline's shocked face, wondering if she realised what Constance's abandoning of her wig meant for *her* future health and wellbeing. 'Tell him to get the train,' said Constance abruptly.

'The train?' John queried.

'Yes, there are plenty of them to Leeds from Scarborough. He can get a taxi from the station. And, if things don't go smoothly,' Constance paused and looked at Pauline again in her mirror. 'We won't have his car to dispose of.'

Pauline's panic was written all over her face. 'Don't worry,' said Constance, smiling at Pauline's response. 'As long as your husband doesn't do anything stupid, you'll both be fine. He's not *likely* to do anything reckless is he?'

Pauline shook her head violently.

'Good. Make the call John.'

Mike picked up instantly and heard the same male voice say, 'Take the train to Leeds. Ring me when you arrive and I'll give further instructions.'

'The train? Why can't I go and get my car?'

'This is not up for discussion Michael. Go and get the train, now!'

Again the call ended abruptly.

With no other choice, Mike picked up his bags and started walking towards the railway station. When he arrived he bought a one way ticket, sat down on bench on the platform and dialled Lisa's number. She answered very quickly.

'Mike! What's happening?'

'I have to go to Leeds. On the train!'

'The train?'

'Well, I don't have a car do I? Pauline took it,' he said tersely.

'Yeah, of course. Sorry.'

'No, I'm sorry. I shouldn't have spoken to you like that. It's not your fault.'

'Never mind,' said Lisa. 'What happens when you get to Leeds?'

'I have to ring him and he'll give me more instructions. I hope they don't get impatient. There's not a train for half an hour.'

'I'm sure they can check the train times Mike. Don't worry. Look, I've got to go now. Ring me as soon as you have your instructions: like you said... you know.'

'Yeah, I know. Just in case.' Mike paused, not knowing what else to say.

'Sorry, I really do have to go, there's someone waiting to talk to me,' said Lisa.

'Oh right, sorry. You go. And Lisa, thanks.'

'Don't be daft. Ring me like I said. And I'll see you tonight.'

'What? Really? Well, I hope so,' but she was gone.

Lisa stared at her mobile phone for a while before murmuring, 'Sorry Mike. It's for your own good.' Then she pushed herself off the wall against which she was leaning, picked up her holdall and walked round the corner into the police station. Five minutes later she was telling Detective Inspector Barton everything she knew about Mike Derbyshire and the abduction of his wife Pauline. She knew nothing of the murder of Peter Adams and the DI did not enlighten her. Just as she finished telling Barton about Mike's instructions to catch the train to Leeds, the door flew open and DC Ashworth burst into the room.

'Ah! Impeccable timing as usual Ashworth. Is DC Pullman upstairs?'

'As far as I know sir,' replied the still green-looking detective.

'Right go and fetch him – he's getting the next train to Leeds. Oh, and give him a good description of Mike Derbyshire on your way back down.'

'Sir?'

'I'll explain later, just go and get him.'

When Ashworth was gone, the DI turned back to Lisa. 'DC Ashworth and I will be driving to Leeds, can you come with us? Don't worry, I'll keep you well away from the action - if there is any; you'll be perfectly safe, but when Mike rings you with his next set of instructions I need to hear them straight away. Can't risk your not being able to get through to us or anything like that.'

Lisa agreed immediately.

'Good,' said Barton. 'Come on, we'll meet DC Ashworth and Pullman at the bottom of the stairs, and get straight off.'

'Shall I bring my bag? Or leave it here?'

'Bring it with you. I wouldn't trust anyone who works in here.'

Lisa laughed, unsure whether DI Barton was serious or not and picked up her bag.

As soon as the DC's arrived the Inspector said, 'Right Pullman, do you know what Mr Derbyshire looks like?'

'Yes sir - if DC Ashworth's description is accurate.'

'Good. I want you to keep a discreet eye on Mr Derbyshire. Right now he's on the platform at the station, waiting for the next train to Leeds. Stay with him. He doesn't know you, so you shouldn't have any trouble.'

'Yes sir,' replied Pullman, hesitating before adding, 'Sir?'

'What is it Pullman?'

'Any idea what time I'll be back? Only me and the wife have tickets for t' theatre tonight. It's her birthday and I promised...'

'DC Pullman,' snarled the Inspector. 'A man's – and a woman's – life may be in danger, and you're worried about missing a date with your wife at the theatre?'

'Yes sir. Sorry sir. I'll let her know we might have to give it a miss.'

'You do that,' growled Barton, before remembering the strain his recent trip to Scotland was putting on his own marriage. Then he added more softly. 'Tell her you'll take her away for the weekend, if you don't make it back in time tonight. I'll sign off your overtime to pay for it.'

DC Ashworth coughed and spluttered, as though choking on a whole chicken.

'Die quietly Ashworth,' said the Inspector. 'Right Pullman, you get off to the station and stay in touch. Ashworth, let's get on our way.'

'You OK to drive, constable?' asked DI Barton as they approached the unmarked BMW that was to take them to Leeds. 'You still look a bit green round the gills.'

'Yes sir. When the crime scene guys showed up at Peter Adams' house, they called me into the kitchen to show me something, and I'm afraid the red pheasant curry I had last night made a reappearance.'

'Not all over the crime scene I hope?'

'No sir, on that fuchsia bush again. Very colourful now, it is.'

'So what did they want to show you?'

'Nothing sir. Said the blood spatter reminded one of them of a group of Polynesian islands he'd been to on holiday. Bloody comedians – heard I'd already been sick, and wanted to see if they could make me do it again.'

Before the Inspector could offer any sympathy or otherwise, Lisa interrupted. 'Blood spatter? What blood spatter and who's Peter Adams?'

The Inspector gave the constable a look of exasperation. 'It seems that Peter Adams is, or was, Pauline Derbyshire's boyfriend. I'm afraid that the people Mike is meeting, really do mean business. I'll drive,' added Barton, snatching the keys from Ashworth. 'Put Lisa's bag in the boot and then get in the back. You can sit in the front with me Lisa. It doesn't look like DC Ashworth is going to be up for scintillating conversation.

As they pulled away, Ashworth's phone rang. He listened and then ended the call. 'That was Pullman sir. There's only one other person waiting on the platform for the Leeds train and he answers to the description I gave him of Mike Derbyshire, so we're all set there.'

DI Barton replied with a simple 'Good', before lapsing into silence until they were well out of Scarborough on the A64, driving as quickly as the traffic would allow. Then he rang DI Bill Jackson in Leeds, explained what was going on, and asked for an armed response team to be on standby. Finishing the call he glanced across at Lisa and saw the worried look on her face, 'Don't worry,' he said. 'Mike'll be fine. They don't know we're coming, and Mike can't give us away because he doesn't know either. You did the right thing Lisa. Then, looking in the rear view mirror he saw his DC sitting with his eyes closed, and winked at Lisa.

'So what was in this Red Pheasant Curry then Ashworth?' As the DC stirred himself, Barton added, 'Quite the gourmet chef our DC Ashworth is, Lisa. Isn't that right Ashworth?'

Accepting the praise, the DC replied with obviously false modesty, 'I've been known to dabble sir.'

'So go on then, what was in this gastronomic delight that you deposited on that unsuspecting fuchsia?'

Ashworth sat himself up and leaned forward, so that the two in front could hear clearly.

'Well, pheasant, obviously.'

'Obviously' replied Barton.

'And fresh root ginger – has to be fresh mind – garlic, cardamom pods, bay leaves, cloves, cinnamon, coriander, cumin. All the

135

usual suspects really,' said Ashworth nonchalantly. 'Oh, and paprika,' he added.

'Oh, of course,' said Barton. 'You can't forget the paprika. I suppose that's what makes it a *red* pheasant curry. So how do you cook it all?'

Ashworth had gone pale. 'Do you mind if I don't talk about it now sir? I don't think travelling in the back of the car is agreeing with me.'

'Bloody hell, Ashworth, if you're going to be sick again, wind the window down and stick your head out. We haven't got time to stop. Ashworth sat back again and stared blankly out of the window. DI Barton winked again at Lisa and smiled. She smiled back. It had worked: Barton had taken her mind off the trouble her friend was in - at least temporarily.

As they entered the outskirts of Leeds and began to negotiate the numerous roundabouts DC Ashworth's phone rang as DC Pullman announced the prompt arrival of Mike's train in Leeds. There was anxious silence in the car until Lisa's mobile phone rang.

CHAPTER 16

Laughing Chinaman/Long Journey to China/Fish Pie/Bull Terrier

'Hi Lisa, it's me.'

'Mike! You all right?'

'Yeah, the train was on time and I've rung and got my instructions. I have to get a taxi to the corner of Sweet Street and Springwell Road, then I have to get out of the taxi and ring them again.'

'Sweet Street and Springwell Road?' Lisa repeated for DI Barton's benefit.

'Yeah, that's right.'

'OK, got it. You take care. Bye!' said Lisa, leaving Mike looking at his phone wondering why she'd cut him off so quickly. Mary Berry was in danger of over mixing the cake she was working on in his stomach. He was scared and had wanted a bit of reassurance from Lisa. Instead she'd cut him off like she didn't want to know anymore. Perhaps that was it. Perhaps she'd realised that she really shouldn't be mixed up in his mess. After all, what good could come of it as far as she was concerned?

He approached the line of taxis outside the station, got in the first one available and gave the driver the address he'd been given. He had to get going before he got too scared to carry on, and before whoever it was decided he was taking too long.

*   *   *

Pauline Derbyshire found herself sitting on a pew at the back of a large disused red brick church. What little light there was, had to fight its way through the narrow arched plain-glass windows, covered in cobwebs and protected by metal grills, high up the walls. She had no idea where she was – she was too cold and too frightened to care. She'd forgotten her abductors' names, but was too frightened to ask, and perhaps was better off not knowing. At least they'd taken the duct tape off her mouth.

The man had just ended a call to Mike, 'He's on his way.'

'Excellent,' said the woman. 'So, Pauline, what do you think of the place?' There's no point in screaming. There isn't a soul around for miles. Not another building around for that matter. Probably a mistake to buy the place really. I had planned to knock it down and build a "super casino" on the site, but Gordon Brown kiboshed all that. Still, I'm sure it's nothing that a bit of palm greasing won't sort out. In the meantime it's a handy place to have... for *private* meetings – like ours.'

138

Pauline shuffled on the hard wooden pew, trying to get a bit more comfortable.

'Not very comfortable are they?' commented Constance. 'I think they were designed that way to keep the congregation awake. But I don't suppose you feel much like dozing off do you? You must be terrified. All alone in a deserted church with two… well us. But what am I doing rambling on like this? We have preparations to make. Hope for the best, but plan for the worst: isn't that what they say? John, give the Laughing Chinaman a ring. Tell him we might have a couple of customers for his "Long Journey to China".'

While the man made the call, Pauline sat with her hands clasped on her lap looking down at the floor, but listened intently, aware that the woman's eyes were on her the whole time. As soon as the man had finished the call, the woman said, 'How rude we are John, introducing the Chinaman into our conversation without explaining who he is to our guest. Tell her would you please? And try not to frighten her too much.' The woman paused before adding, 'Oh, what the Hell? Frighten her as much as you like.' Then she wandered off up the centre aisle looking around her as if making plans for the building.

The man sat himself down uncomfortably close to Pauline, smiled a tight-lipped smile, and began his explanation, 'The Laughing Chinaman is so called because he enjoys his work so much, that he laughs almost continuously while he's doing it, and because he is of distant Chinese decent. His name is... well you don't need to know his name, but it's Chinese – although *he* doesn't look it. He looks more like a bull terrier – even when he's laughing. And like I said he laughs a lot.'

Pauline was puzzled, but was too frightened to speak.

'Oh, sorry,' said the man. 'I haven't explained what he does have I? He's our disposal engineer. He disposes of things or people that have...*disappointed* us. He does this for nothing – because he enjoys it so much. And we trust him to do a good job, because by the time he's finished with his customers they are totally unrecognisable, and it's as much in his interest as it is in ours, that they are never found. "The Long Journey to China" is simply our code for what the Chinaman does. We would hardly want to be overheard telling the Chinaman we want him to torture and dispose of somebody would we?'

Pauline continued to look at the floor, her knuckles whitening as she clasped her hands tighter. The man leaned in even closer. 'Would you like to know what he does? No? Well I'll tell you. Just in general terms so that you know roughly what to expect, should you or your husband... disappoint us.' The man paused but did not sit back. Pauline could feel his breath on her cheek as his voice dropped to almost a whisper. 'He likes knives,' he said. 'Well almost anything with a sharp blade really - or a sharp point. He likes points as well. And then there's heat – he likes hot things; likes to make patterns on your skin with them. That's apart from all the usual sexual depravities you'd expect someone in his line of work to possess. Apparently he likes to indulge his sexual deviations before the torture begins. Then he rewards you with a meal, lulling you into a false sense of security if that's the right phrase. Making you think that he's merely going to keep you as his sex slave. Like I said "false sense of security" is not necessarily the right phrase. But if you knew what was coming next, you'd understand what I mean. Now where was I? Oh yes, the meal. If he's really... appreciating you, then the food will be good and wholesome and will give you the energy, if not the inclination, to keep satisfying him: if not then you'll get the fish pie!' The man paused again, giving Pauline the opportunity to try to unravel what he meant. After a few moments he continued. 'I can see that you're wondering why the fish pie is so significant. Well I'll tell you. It will have some dodgy prawns in it. Of course you won't know this, and I'm told that his fish pie is particularly delicious. But after you've eaten it, he will strap you to a steel chair bolted to the floor in the middle of an empty room; your arms tied behind your back. He will then leave you for a few hours – watching you via the CCTV mounted in a corner of the room. When you start vomiting he'll come back, apologise for the effects of his food, and say that it can't be nice sitting there covered in vomit. Then he'll hose you down with high-powered ice cold water. Then he'll strip you off and turn up the air conditioning and leave you to shiver yourself dry. After that, he starts with the knives.'

The man finally sat back and was quiet. Pauline's sobs suddenly burst from her. She leant forward, elbows on her knees, her hands covering her face. She felt a sharp smack on the side of her head that nearly knocked her off the pew. Then she felt a hand in her hair pulling her head back sharply, the woman's face was almost touching her own. 'Be quiet,' the woman said. 'Stop your blubbing. I can't abide weak women. Believe me it'll be a lot worse than John's made it sound. *Now* you know what will happen to you and your husband if either of you mess up, don't you?

Tears streamed down her face but Pauline said nothing. 'I said, "Don't you"?' growled the woman.

Pauline heard herself whisper 'Yes' in reply.

*   *   *

As soon as Lisa finished her call from Mike, DI Barton pulled over into a bus stop.

'Detective Constable, you'd better get in the front and programme your girlfriend.'

Lisa looked puzzled and not a little offended.

DC Ashworth leaned forward, 'Don't worry Lisa, he's not insulting you. He means the SATNAV. He refers to it as my girlfriend, because he says they always end up telling me where to go.'

Lisa laughed, 'Is that true?'

Both policeman answered, 'Yes.'

'Oh, I've got another one Ashworth. I've decided I'll call your girlfriends "bus conductresses".'

Ashworth sighed, 'Go on then, Sir. Why?'

'Because they always tell you where to get off!' Barton chuckled. Lisa laughed and told him he was cruel. Ashworth sighed once more, dropped back into his seat and said, 'A right comedian you are... Sir.'

'I'm glad you appreciate my sense of humour,' said Barton, still chuckling.

'Well, you can stay where you are constable,' said Lisa. 'I can programme your girlfriend. Sorry, I mean the SATNAV.' She reached forward and punched in the address Mike had given her. Sitting back she turned towards DI Barton. 'Inspector?'

'Yes Lisa?'

'What are you going to do, once you know where Mike is actually going? I mean, are you going to let him actually meet these people?'

'We can't Lisa. We know these people are killers, and they already have one hostage. Mike would simply be another one. Once we are certain they have given Mike his final instructions, we'll arrest him.'

'Then what?'

'Then we'll let them know that we have all their exits covered and ask them to give themselves up.'

'And if they don't?'

'We'll cross that bridge when we come to it. But at least Mike will be safe. Now I have to make a phone call.' Reaching forward, Barton pressed a couple of buttons on the mobile phone mounted on the dashboard and waited for his call to be picked up. The phone was answered swiftly.

'Hello Dick, what's happening? We're all ready at this end.'

'Hi Bill. Our man's been instructed to get a taxi to the corner of Sweet Street and Springwell Road. No doubt he'll be given more instructions then. So we need you close but don't let him see you. He has no idea that we're following, and I haven't a clue what he'd do if he found out. We have one of our own officers following in another taxi, and SATNAV says we're only five minutes away ourselves.'

'OK,' came the response.' I'll let you know where we park up. See you soon.'

'Cheers,' said DI Barton ending the call.

'Dick?' said Lisa. 'That really your name?'

'What's wrong with Dick as a name?' replied the Inspector.' But no it's not. It's a nickname. Had it since school – after Dick Barton.'

Lisa shook her head. 'No, never heard of him.'

'Really?' gasped the Inspector. 'You've never hear of Dick Barton - Special Agent?'

DC Ashworth laughed out loud. 'See sir? I'm not the only one.'

'Youth of today – no culture,' sighed Barton. 'No wonder the world's in such a state.'

Lisa looked round at the DC in the back and they both rolled their eyes, before DC Ashworth pointed out, 'My girlfriend says our destination is just around the corner sir. Perhaps we'd better pull up here?'

'My thoughts exactly constable' replied the DI pulling over.

'Sir, there is an alternative to just arresting Mr Derbyshire and then letting them know we're on to them.'

'Enlighten me constable.'

'Well, they've never met Derbyshire, right?'

Barton looked at Lisa for confirmation. She nodded in rely.

'Go on,' said the inspector.

'So someone could take his place.'

'With what aim constable?'

'Well, we could tag the bag with the money in it electronically, so that we could follow it. *And* we'd have someone on the inside if things kicked off.'

Barton looked in the rear view mirror to address his Constable. 'I know we've all been on these courses where they tell you that no idea is a bad idea but trust me Martin, that's a bad idea. Nice of you to volunteer – I presume you were volunteering - but these people are killers remember, and letting them out of wherever they are, and doubling the number of hostages they have, is not a good idea. Thanks anyway.'

The DC slumped back in the seat and stared out of the window. 'I suppose so,' he said sullenly.

DI Barton's mobile rang. He removed it from its holder, 'Hi, Bill. You in position?'

'Yes, we're on Atkinson Street, just round the corner.'

'Good, we're on Wellington Street – just round the other corner. Hang on, we've got another call coming in. Stay on the line.'

Lisa's phone was ringing. Barton nodded for her to answer it.

CHAPTER 17

Murdered/Scotland/A Black Eye

'Lisa, it's me.'

'Mike! Are you all right?' She held her phone so that Barton could listen in.

'Yeah, so far. I've just rung them again. I have to walk round the corner into Atkinson Street, take the first on the left, the second on the right and then I'll see a large area of wasteland with a big old church on the other side. I have to ring them when I'm there. I have a feeling they'll come and pick me up then. There's no point in making me walk again.'

'Atkinson Street? You have to walk down Atkinson Street? Hang on a minute can you?' Lisa placed her hand over the microphone on her phone and turned to DI Barton. 'Did you hear that? Mike is going down Atkinson Street. He'll see the other Police team!'

Barton was already speaking into his phone. 'He's coming your way Bill. Get out of there, now!'

'Lisa! Are you still there?'

'Yes sorry Mike. Someone came to my desk. Had to get rid of them. Are you on your way?'

'Yes, I'm just turning into Atkinson Street. Shit! There are two Police cars and vans! Oh no, it's OK they're haring past with their sirens going. I thought they were here for me for a minute. Can you hear me?'

'Just about,' replied Lisa just as the same police vehicles drove screaming past her.

'Where are you Lisa? I can hear Police sirens. Same as the ones that have just gone past me.'

Lisa waited for the sirens to fade, using the time to think of an answer. 'That's better. I've just stepped outside the office. Said I'd follow that colleague out. He's having a ciggy break and he needs to discuss something with me.' Barton nodded his approval of her quick thinking and Lisa carried on. 'But never mind that. You sure you're OK?'

'Yeah. As OK as I can be. To be honest I'm starting to get a bit fed up with all this running around. Why can't they just meet me and pick up the money?'

'I don't know Mike. Perhaps that *is* what going to happen at the church. Sounds like it's in the middle of nowhere. Just do what they tell you and let me know as soon as you know what's happening.'

'OK. Oh!'

'What?'

'I've just thought; if they *do* pick me up how will I let you know where they're taking me? They're hardly likely to allow me to make a phone call.'

'Let me think,' said Lisa. She put her hand over the mobile phone and turned to Barton, opening her eyes wide, pleading for an idea.

Barton simply frowned, and D.C. Ashworth took the opportunity to lean forward excitedly and say, 'Tell him to leave his phone on after he's spoken to you. Tell him you might be able to hear what they say.'

Lisa looked doubtful, but Barton nodded and said, 'Might as well: it's all we've got.'

Lisa repeated the idea to Mike who seemed quite taken with it, before ending the call.

'It won't work. He'll have to keep his phone in his pocket and I won't be able to hear a thing,' Lisa told the two policemen.

'Of course not,' said Ashworth still leaning forward. 'But that doesn't matter to us does it? We'll be watching anyway. Won't we sir?'

'Exactly Constable. We'll make a detective out of you yet.' Then Barton spoke into his mobile phone. 'You still there Bill?'

'Yep. Your man saw us but I don't think he suspected anything.'

'No, he didn't. Just thought you were going somewhere in a hurry. Where are you now?'

'Pulled up around the corner from you.'

'Good. Stay there. It looks like Derbyshire is going to be picked up in front of a church on some wasteland round the corner. We'll try to keep an eye on things from a distance.'

'OK Dick. We'll sit tight.'

Barton put his mobile back in his pocket, started the car up and followed the instructions Mike had been given. They soon came across the derelict wasteland he'd mentioned and could see him making his way across it, sticking to roads that still criss-crossed the area. They could see a large church standing alone on the far side of the open land. The Inspector saw a back alley that would give them a good view and he reversed into it to wait for developments.

As Mike walked towards the church he wondered if Lisa had realised yet that her idea of his leaving his phone on wouldn't work. There was no way she'd be able to hear anything. He was on his own now. All he could now was follow their instructions and hope for the best. He reached the church, its red bricks darkened by the city's industrial past, and looked around – there as no one in sight. There was a low brick wall surrounding the church only a few feet from the church walls. Mike stepped through a gap in the wall that had once held a gate, and into the porch in front of the large wooden doors and rang the number.

*   *   *

'He's ringing them now' said D.I Barton. All three occupants of the car watched intently and waited for Lisa's phone to ring.

150

It didn't.

Instead they watched as Mike turned, opened the door of the church, and walked inside.

'Oh my God!' said Barton. 'They must be inside.' He picked up his mobile and rang Bill Jackson. 'Bill, they're in the church. You'd better get a bit closer where you can see what's going on. Ashworth and I will take a closer look. Look after Lisa, will you? She'll be waiting for you.' Then turning his head towards her, he said, 'Right Lisa, out you get. You're not coming any closer.'

'But...'

'No buts. He's not going to ring again. Not if they're in there, so come on, out you get.'

Lisa opened the door and stepped out of the BMW and watched as it wound its way slowly across the wasteland to the suddenly sinister looking church.

DI Barton looked in the rear view mirror. 'Right, Martin,' he said. 'We're just scanning the place OK? No heroics. Someone's already been murdered and you'll get more than a black eye if you go barging in. And how would I explain that to your current bus conductress?'

'Yes sir,' replied the DC

DI Barton smiled. His DC had acquired a reputation for charging into dangerous situations. So far it had paid off, got him a couple of commendations, but today was not the day for such recklessness. The inspector stopped the car a good fifty metres away from the church to avoid the engine noise being noticed by anyone inside and they walked together towards the building.

'Let's have look round the back,' said Barton. 'They must have driven here. Their car must be somewhere.' Sure enough, round the back of the church they came across a gleaming black Mercedes with dark tinted windows. Barton signalled for Ashworth to follow and went to the far side of the car. He knelt down by the rear wheel, looked round on the ground, found what he was looking for and then unscrewed the dust cap and began letting the air out of the tyre. He nodded at Ashworth, who followed suit. As they walked back to their BMW, Barton said, 'We'll get back to DI Jackson and decide what to do next. We'll have to get both of the church's exits covered with the armed response team and then we'll let whoever's in the church know that we're here. Hopefully they'll realise they have no alternative other than to give themselves up.'

They got in the car and Barton drove in silence. He had a bad feeling about the situation. Suddenly the arguments he'd had with his wife since he'd got back from Scotland seemed ridiculously trivial. He had to try to put things right. Pulling up next to DI Jackson, who was leaning on his car talking to Lisa and some of his own officers, Barton got out the car, held up his hand with his fingers spread to ask for five minutes on his own. As he walked away from the group he dialled his wife's mobile number. It went to voicemail. 'Bollocks!' he thought, then said, 'Hi, it's me. Just ringing to say sorry. I'll speak to you later.' He paused before finally adding, 'I love you, bye.'

Returning to DI Jackson and his officers, Barton quickly brought them all up to date with the situation and concluded with his plan, such as it was. 'OK Bill, I suggest we split your armed men to cover front and back. Make sure they all have a good view of the exits but stay well covered.'

Bill Jackson interrupted, 'Grannies and sucking eggs are coming to mind Dick. These men know what they're doing.'

'Yeah, sorry, I know. Just don't want it blowing up in our faces. *You* know how dangerous these people are more than I do. Anyway, once you're in position, I'll knock politely and let them know we're here.'

'And I'm sure they'll invite you in for tea and biscuits,' said Jackson.

'Or just blow a few holes in the door. On second thoughts, can I borrow your phone Lisa? I presume you have Mike's number in there.'

'Yes, of course,' replied Lisa handing Barton her mobile.

'What's he in as?'

'Der! Mike Derbyshire!' came the reply.

Pullman and Ashworth laughed.

'All right, all right. I was just checking. There could have been other Mike's in here,' said Barton as he scrolled through the contact list to find Mike Derbyshire's name. 'I think I'll ring them from a safe distance, once you're in position. Everybody clear?

'Everybody nodded or grunted a 'Yes sir.'

'Right, let's get going,' said Barton. 'You stay here Lisa, in the spare car, with that officer. He'll look after you.'

Looking at the officer indicated, Lisa doubted that – he was at least two inches shorter than her and didn't look old enough to smoke or intelligent enough not to, but she nodded her agreement anyway. Then she watched as the cars and vans weaved their way around the potholes that scarred the neglected roads which eventually led them to the church.

Her guardian officer took out a packet of cigarettes and offered one to Lisa. 'Thought so,' she said to herself, declining the offer. Then she stepped away as the young policeman lit up and watched as the armed officers got into position and DI Barton got out of his car about twenty metres from the front of the church and held her mobile phone to his ear.

CHAPTER 18

National Anthem/Racehorse/Russia

As Mike had entered the church and looked around, trying to adjust to the half-light, a powerful hand had gripped his throat almost crushing his larynx, and as he struggled for breath another hand had ripped the holdall from his grasp. The hand on his throat then swung him round before shoving him away violently, throwing him down on to the cold stone floor.

'Get up and sit next to your wife,' commanded a booming female voice.

Mike got to his knees and looked around.

He saw Pauline sitting hunched up on a pew nearby, and tried to smile. He didn't know why; there was obviously nothing to smile about. The female voice boomed out again. 'I said sit next to your wife!'

Mike looked in the direction of the voice and saw a red-haired woman standing in the pulpit at the opposite end of the aisle.

She didn't look like a vicar.

As he struggled to his feet and moved towards Pauline, the woman stepped down from the pulpit and walked towards him.

'Is it all there John?' she asked.

'Well, there's over nineteen grand,' replied the tall well-built man who'd nearly throttled Mike.

'Good,' replied the woman. 'It's nice to meet you at last, Mike. I'd like to say that I've heard such a lot about you, but I'm afraid your wife has been a little taciturn since we picked her up. Thank you for bringing me my money. My name is Constance Tyler by the way. And the man standing behind you, who gave you such a warm welcome, is my close friend and associate John Kilgallon. I may as well tell you that I don't mind telling you our names because you won't get the chance to tell anyone about us.'

'What?' shouted Mike '*He* said everything would be all right if I brought you the money.'

'And so it will be – for me. But I'm afraid I really can't let you go. You could identify us quite easily.'

'But it's too late to worry about that,' reasoned Mike. 'You were seen in Ayton-le-Dale, and at the hospital yesterday.'

'That's true Michael. You don't mind if I call you Michael instead of Mike, do you? I think it sounds more appropriate in a church. We *were* seen yesterday but Mrs Johnston and the people in the Pub saw a woman with long dark hair and a man wearing an unusual pair of glasses. Not a woman with short red hair and a man with twenty-twenty vision. And of course, we both have over fifty witnesses we could call on to swear we never left Leeds yesterday. So you see, only you and your wife are a definite risk to us.'

'But that's not f...'

'Not fair, Michael? Please don't say it's not fair. We're not in the playground now. Anyway, what's not fair? You stole my money – not from me directly, but you still stole it – so you deserve to be punished. Would you like to tell your husband what's going to happen to you both Pauline?'

Pauline raised her head, 'Piss off!' she spat.

'Goodness me Pauline! That's no way to talk in a house of God. Michael, do you think you could calm your wife down? She seems to be a little upset.'

'What the hell do you expect?' yelled Mike. 'You've just told us you're going to kill us.'

'That's true,' replied Constance, smiling. 'I can see how that could be upsetting. Of course it's more upsetting for Pauline because she's had a detailed description of how you're both going to suffer before you die. Isn't that right Pauline?'

The reminder took away Pauline's defiance again, and she simply nodded.

'You're going to torture us? How sick are you people?'

'Not us exactly, our...contractor will be doing the torture, and I'm afraid he does that because he enjoys it, and he doesn't charge us a penny! We call him the "Laughing Chinaman" because... well perhaps your wife can tell you when she's not quite so upset. He should be here in a few minutes. Then we can all be on our way.' Constance signalled to John to bring the holdall to her and she looked inside and smiled. 'A lot of effort for a relatively small amount of money. But as I said yesterday, this was personal. And I suppose I can put it towards that racehorse I have my eye on.'

Mike was at a total loss. Pauline was sobbing quietly beside him and there was no way out. She'd done nothing wrong and she was going to be tortured alongside him. He stretched his arm around her, and whispered, 'I'm sorry Pauline, I....'

Pauline leapt to her feet. 'Sorry? You're sorry? Is that the best you can do?' she screamed, as she slapped his face and then began to pummel his head with her fists. Nobody did anything to stop her. Even Mike sat still as best he could and took the blows. He deserved it. Eventually Pauline ran out of steam and slumped down on the pew.

Mike looked Constance in the eye mustering all the courage he could, just to speak to her. 'Can't you let her go? She won't tell anyone about you. She won't describe you to the Police or anything. She'll promise, won't you Pauline?'

Pauline ignored her husband, and sat with her head in her hands, weeping.

Mike tried again. 'It's not her fault! She had nothing to do with taking the money. You can do anything you like to me just let her go!'

'Very noble of you Michael,' replied Constance. 'But we, or rather the Laughing Chinaman, is already going to do anything he likes to you, so your offer is not much of a bargaining ploy.' Constance paused for a moment as if reconsidering. 'Tell you what, Michael. I'll give you a challenge, and if you can meet it, I'll let Pauline go.'

John Kilgallon's face showed total confusion.

Constance continued, 'If you can sing the National Anthem... no that's too easy. If you can sing the National Anthem of *Russia*...no that's too easy. If you can sing the National Anthem of Russia *backwards*, then I'll let her go. Hell! I'll let both of you go.'

John Kilgallon smiled and shook his head. Sometimes his boss had a sick sense of humour.

Before Mike could respond his mobile phone started ringing. The smile left Constance's face. 'Your trousers seem to be ringing Michael,' she said flatly, giving John Kilgallon a menacing look, and adding, 'Getting careless, John.'

Kilgallon dragged Mike to his feet and held his hand out without saying a word. Mike stuck his hand in his pocket and pulled out his phone and handed it to Kilgallon who passed it straight to Constance. As she looked at the display, and smiled briefly she said, 'Lisa? Who's Lisa, Michael? Don't tell me you've been playing away as well?' Then she rejected the call as Michael looked at his wife wondering what the 'as well' had meant. But Pauline had retreated completely within herself and did not lift her head.

'Oh, didn't you know, Michael? Pauline has, or rather had, a boyfriend.'

Whilst her use of the past tense simply confirmed John's suspicions about why Constance had gone back into Peter Adams' house, it hit Pauline like a thunderbolt. She shot to her feet, her screams echoing around the cavernous church. John stepped behind her and pushed her firmly back down on to the pew.

'Well, what did you expect me to do Pauline?' said Constance, 'I could hardly leave your boyfriend alive. If he thought as much about you, as you obviously did about him, then he would be very dangerous. He'd want answers. He'd keep pushing. No I couldn't risk it. If it's any consolation it was very quick. Much quicker than... well, you know.'

Mike looked at Pauline, 'Don't you dare even ask!' she snarled before he had chance to say anything.

'But...' Mike was interrupted by his mobile phone ringing in Constance's hand. She looked at the display. 'Lisa, again!' she said. 'Isn't she persistent?' Again she rejected the call. 'Let's just sit quietly and wait for the Chinaman, shall we? No need for you two to air your dirty linen in public. Not in the house of God.'

*   *   *

Outside the church DI Barton was feeling frustrated. He'd rung twice and been cut off both times. They'd have to knock on the door after all. 'Can I do it sir?' asked DC Ashworth.

Barton looked at DI Jackson a couple of yards away. Jackson shrugged his shoulders in response. 'OK,' said Barton. 'But that's all you do. Knock on the door and tell them who we are.'

DC Ashworth smiled and walked briskly into the church porch. He thumped the door three times and then shouted, 'This is the Police. We have the place surrounded. Come out with your hands up and no one will get hurt.'

Then he turned round and walked back to his Inspector with a huge smile on his face. 'I've always wanted to say that,' he said.

Barton could hear DI Jackson chuckling, but he didn't look at him. Instead he said, 'Good grief, Ashworth! What was that? This isn't the ruddy Wild West! Now go back and knock on the door again and ask them to answer the phone the next time I ring. Tell them we're Lisa! And hope they don't start blowing holes in the doors.'

The DC walked back to the door, thumped it three times again and shouted, 'Answer the phone when Lisa rings! We are Lisa! I mean, we are using Lisa's phone!' Realising he'd not quite got it right, he added, 'Just answer the soddin' phone will you?' and walked quickly back to his DI, who was shaking his head again.

*   *   *

Inside the church, Constance strode over to Mike and slapped his face hard, once with her left and once with her right hand so that his head whipped one way then the other. 'What have you done?' she demanded. 'How have the Police got your girlfriend's phone and how do they know we're here?'

'I don't know,' replied Mike, holding his face, 'really I don't. I only met her last night.'

'I don't want your life story,' growled Constance. 'What's going on?'

'I don't know - really. Like I said, I only met her last night and we had a few drinks, and I ended up telling her everything. She told me I should go to the Police, but I didn't! I swear! I didn't!'

'So how do they know we're here?'

'She must have told them. I've been ringing her to tell her what's been happening, so that she *could* go the Police if anything happened to me.'

Constance slapped Mike's face again and nodded for John to bring her handbag from a pew across the aisle. She reached inside and removed a gun. 'Well, something *has* happened to you,' she said, as she pointed the weapon at a spot just between Mike's eyes.

Then his mobile phone rang again. Constance ignored it. 'The only reason I'm not going to kill you now,' she explained, 'is because I know what the Chinaman will do to you.'

Then she answered the phone.

CHAPTER 19

New Cook/Cairngorms/Boston Promenade Concert Orchestra

Mike stared at the gun pointing at his head. He was sure that thing on the end of it must be a silencer, though it seemed a little unnecessary since everyone could see the gun in her hand and the Police were already outside. He heard the woman speak into *his* phone, 'Hello, is that Lisa or the cowboy who has us surrounded?'

He knew he should have kept listening but he was transfixed by the nozzle of the silencer inches away from his face. Panic enveloped him. His mind started to race. How the hell had he gotten into this mess?

A little over twenty-four hours ago he'd been setting off on his usual weekend bike ride. He'd even had the usual argument about money with Pauline. Everything had been fine. She'd have done a bit of cleaning or ironing or something and would have had his roast dinner more or less ready for him when he got home. But hang on a minute. She had a boyfriend. At least she'd had a boyfriend! It sounded like he was an 'ex' in every sense of the word. But why had she had a boyfriend? What was wrong with their marriage? What was wrong with *him*? Suddenly, totally irrationally, this seemed to be the most important thing on Mike's mind. The woman with his phone had moved away so that Mike couldn't hear what she was saying although she didn't sound very happy. He turned to Pauline, 'You had a boyfriend!' he hissed.

'What?'

'I said, "You had a boyfriend"!'

'I know what you said. I just don't know why you're bringing it up now.'

Mike was in no mood to be put off. 'Because I'm your bloody husband,' he whispered. 'And I've a right to know if you were playing around.'

'Playing around! Don't you dare call it that! It was a lot more than that. I'd left you remember – before you got me into,' she paused and waved a hand around, finishing with 'THIS!'

'Never mind "This"! You had a boyfriend before *this* happened. I want to know why!'

'Because we had nothing in common. You are the most boring man I've ever met!'

'Boring? Me?'

'Yes you! Take yesterday for instance…'

'Yesterday! Yesterday wasn't boring! Yesterday I found twenty grand. Remember?'

'How could I forget? But only because you were out on your weekly bike ride. You go every Sunday, come rain or shine in your lycra shorts and with your water bottle topped up to *just* the right level of hydrating fluids. Nothing can stop that happening.'

'That's not true. I took you away for a spontaneous romantic weekend not long ago.'

'Not long ago? It was two years ago! And you won it in a raffle at work. And only you could think a weekend in the Cairngorms in the middle of winter could be romantic.'

'Not romantic? The scenery was fantastic: all those snow covered mountains.'

'It *could* have been romantic I admit that, but your real reason for going was to hire a mountain bike and go off on your own. And when there was too much snow you spent the whole weekend sulking, watching rugby on the tele. It was about as romantic as a wet Wednesday in Wetwang! And last Christmas you bought me a Christmas album by the Boston Promenade Concert Orchestra because *you* wanted the music from "How the Grinch Stole Christmas"!'

'I thought *you'd* like it!' protested Mike.'

'Like it? Why on earth would I like it? It's a kids film! Why would I want the soundtrack? Everything was always about you.'

'No it wasn't. That's ridiculous.'

'Yes it was. Every wall in the house is painted "Magnolia", because you like it!

'You like it as well!'

'Yes I do. But not on every bloody wall! Like I said, boring!' Pauline paused and turned to look at John Kilgallon who was smiling, obviously enjoying the show she and Mike were putting on. Constance was at the far end of the aisle still busy on the phone. 'I can't believe I'm having this conversation, now of all times, but you asked for it,' she said. 'Every night you watch the same programmes on television. After you've had the same meals on the same nights every week. Roast on Sunday; same with leftovers on Monday, pork chops Tuesday, pie on Wednesday, lasagne on Thursday – very exotic for you that, and fish on Fridays. God knows why you insist on fish on Fridays. You're about as religious as a cockroach. And then of course curry on Saturday, washed down with precisely three hundred and thirty milli- bloody-litres of lager. Same... week after interminable week. And who had it to cook it every time? Well, it wasn't you was it? Oh no. You had to catch up with the day's news, while I was in the kitchen – as if you'd find any in the Daily Mail. I'll bet when you found my note yesterday morning, your first thought was that you'd have to find a new cook!'

'No it wasn't,' replied Mike truthfully. His first thought had been to count the money; only then had he thought about getting something to eat and gone to the Pub, although he had intended to order a roast as it had been Sunday. 'Anyway, what did this... this boyfriend have that I didn't?'

'Everything!' screamed Pauline. 'He was everything that you aren't! And you've got him killed! You bast...' A hand clamped over her mouth, silencing her. As Mike turned to help his wife, John Kilgallon's other hand swatted him away like a fly and he fell sideways, banging his forehead on the back of the pew in front of them.

Constance had finished her discussion with DI Barton and had appeared at the end of the pew. 'You, get up and keep quiet,' she said to Mike. 'John, you go and check the back door. They say they have that covered as well, and that the "Merc" has two flat tyres.'

While John went off to carry out her bidding, Constance looked at Pauline and Mike. 'I can see why you left him,' she said to Pauline. 'And I do feel sorry for you. Who knows? There may be a way out for you yet. Since the Police know who we are, there is technically no reason for me to give you to the Laughing Chinaman.' Pauline's face didn't flicker, but Mike let out a sigh of relief.

Constance glared at him. 'I was talking to your wife. You're still going to the Chinaman!'

'But...'

'Be quiet!' Constance demanded. 'Another word from you and I'll kill you myself.' Then she turned towards John's advancing footsteps and said, 'Well?'

'They've got the back covered all right. Can't see the flat tyres. They must be on the other side of the car – or they're bluffing. But they've no reason to. I saw three coppers all with rifles pointed at the door.'

'In that case we'll have to leave by the *front* door.'

'How are we going to do that?' asked John.

'We're going to need something to divert their attention. Give me a moment.' As she walked up the aisle, Constance slipped the mobile phone into her bag and removed her gun once more. To Mike, who could only see her back, it looked as though Constance was fiddling with the gun as she walked, and that she then put something in her bag. When she turned around Mike could see that the silencer had been removed, and that she was making a phone call on his mobile. She pointed the gun at Mike and indicated that he should stand up and then move into the aisle.

'Ah, Detective Inspector Lisa.' Constance smiled at her joke and looked Mike in the eyes. 'I'm afraid we need an ambulance,' she said. 'Someone's been shot.'

She pointed the gun at Mike's forehead. His 'fight or flee' instinct was completely overridden by his 'rooted to the spot' instinct. He looked at John, 'You can't let her...' John shrugged his shoulders in response, he could see the light in Constance's eyes and knew nothing he could say would stop her doing whatever she intended. Mike looked at Pauline to plead for him. She looked down at her feet. 'You've no friends here Michael,' said Constance. Sweat ran down Mike's face as he watched Constance's finger begin to squeeze the trigger and he closed his eyes. He didn't see the barrel drop before Constance shot him in the centre of his right knee cap.

Outside, DI Barton and his colleagues heard the gunshot echo around the church, followed swiftly by a blood-curdling scream that went on and on and seemed to pour through every brick of the walls in front of them as though the building itself was crying out in agony. DC Ashworth took half a step towards the church but his Inspector placed a restraining hand on the constable's shoulder. 'What did I tell you about heroics?' he said. Ashworth turned to protest but Barton held up his hand to silence him; he was still listening to his mobile phone.

'I do hope you can hear me above all this noise,' said Constance. 'As I was saying, someone has been shot. Could you be a dear, and call for an ambulance?' She ended the call.

Barton ordered his DC to call for an ambulance and turned to DI Jackson. 'Jesus Bill! What sort of people are they?'

'Desperate. They've already killed once today. Got nothing to lose, I suppose.'

The blood-curdling screams still coming from inside the church seemed to swirl around them in the still air, demanding a response.

'Ambulance is on its way. We going in sir?' asked DC Ashworth slipping his mobile back into his jacket.

'Going in? No, we are not bloody going in. There are still two hostages in there.'

'But…'

'But nothing Constable. There are still two *live* hostages in there. One of them wounded admittedly, but still alive. Dead people don't scream like that.'

The screaming stopped.

*   *   *

Inside the church Constance looked down at Mike as he writhed on the floor and smiled. 'That's better Michael. You really shouldn't scream like that in a church. It's not respectful. John, if he starts screaming again, stand on his knee.'

Mike's mobile phone started ringing, and Constance accepted the call and put the phone to her ear. 'Ah, DI Lisa. Ambulance on its way? Good…. Yes, of course he's still alive. Would you like to hear him screaming again?' Constance made a show of looking disappointed. 'No? Oh well. Never mind. Let us know when the ambulance arrives won't you?' She ended the call once more.

Pauline sat motionless struggling to hold herself together. She wanted to explode from her seat and tear the face off the woman holding them. Not because of what she'd

171

done to her husband, Mike: he could go to Hell. And not just because of what she'd done to Pete, but because of what she was now doing to *her,* taunting her, treating her like she was hers to do with as she wanted, like she was worth nothing to anyone. She looked at Mike, blood oozing between the fingers of his hands holding his knee, tears streaming down his cheeks as he rocked from side to side groaning. She felt sorry for him, like she would be for an injured dog. She slid along the pew and knelt on the floor beside him, avoiding the dark red patch growing ever larger on the stone floor. He paused in his rocking, and looked into her eyes and managed to stop groaning long enough to say, 'Sorry.'

'Too late for that,' said Pauline, struggling to find something to say. Eventually she added, 'At least they've ordered an ambulance for you. That's a good sign.'

'I suppose so,' replied Mike.

Pauline looked down at Mike's leg. Blood was still flowing copiously through his fingers.

'Is there anything we can put on this?' she asked looking at John. John shrugged.

'Don't worry yourself Pauline,' said Constance. 'If he dies, he dies. Surely you don't want him back?'

Pauline leapt to her feet and was about to lunge at Constance when John's arms folded around her and held her firmly. 'You callous little...' she screamed. John's hand covered her mouth and silenced her as Mike's mobile phone ring echoed around the church yet again.

CHAPTER 20

Arrows/Broken Walking Stick/Ireland

'Yes, it's here. You coming out *now?*' said DI Barton.

'Yes we are Inspector. Have the driver park as closely as he can, with the driver's door nearest the church, and then open the back doors. Tell him to leave the keys in the ignition, and walk away from the vehicle. And I want you all to back off. I want no one within a hundred yards when we come out. Let me know when that's done,' said Constance, before ending the call abruptly and addressing Kilgallon. 'OK John, we're on. The ambulance is outside, and we're all getting in. I'll be driving. You'll be in the back with these two.'

'Then what?' asked John.

'Then we drive off.'

'And they follow,' said John.

'I'll insist that they don't of course.'

John looked at Constance as though she had just landed from Mars. Constance acknowledged his concern with a nod and said to Pauline, 'You, sit there and keep still.'

John released Pauline and she dutifully sat down on the pew indicated. Constance took a few steps away; John followed. 'They'll follow, of course they will,' said Constance, 'but at a distance. I'll threaten them so that they at least try to deceive us, and stay far enough back. I was brought up round here John, and I know every street and back alley. Once we've crossed the waste ground outside this place, I'll make a couple of turns and we'll be in a narrow road with cars parked down one side - only room for one car to go in one direction at a time. You'll throw laughing boy out there. The Police won't be able to drive round him and he won't be able to get out of their way, especially after you've shot him in the other knee cap. They'll have to stop to take care of him. Another turn will put us in another road that's just the same. There'll be a car waiting for us. We'll abandon the ambulance there, and the Police will be stuck behind it, once they get past Derbyshire, that is. If we're fast enough we can be out of the immediate area before they have all the exits covered. Then we're off to a safe house while we wait for passports to take us out of the country. I thought we could start with Ireland: with your contacts out there we should be able to disappear long enough to get a long term plan worked out.'

John knew better than to express doubts verbally but his face said it all.

'I know John, it's not perfect, but it's all we have. I'm sorry we've ended up in this mess. All down to my obsession with Stephenson.'

'Just more "slings and arrows", boss that's all. "Outrageous fortune" and all that. I've been in worse situations. You weren't to know that *he'd* have told some bird he'd just met all about it, and that she'd go to the Police.'

Constance smiled and touched John's arm. 'Thanks John. What would I do without your loyalty?'

'Stop it, you'll make me blush. What about her?' he asked looking at Pauline.

Constance made sure Pauline could hear her reply. 'If she doesn't give you any grief in the ambulance, we'll leave her in it for the Police to "rescue". If she misbehaves in any way at all, you'll have to kill her. The Chinaman will be disappointed but you can't please everybody.'

Pauline felt the rage towards the woman who was holding her prisoner, who was treating her like a disposable commodity, building up inside her again. Again she wanted to beat the woman to a pulp. A broken walking stick underneath the pew in front of her caught her eye. Made of wood, the broken end was jagged and sharp. She could do some damage with that. She didn't give it a second thought. She reached down under the pew, banging into it with her shoulder. John and Constance turned towards the noise in time to see Pauline climbing to her feet brandishing the broken walking stick like a cudgel. As Kilgallon confronted her, Pauline raised her right arm to strike with her weapon but with a look of condescending disdain and a speed of movement Pauline had never seen before, he simply grabbed her arm with his left hand, and twisted her wrist so that she dropped the stick and screamed in pain. Then he raised his right hand to strike but paused before letting it fall to his side.

'Ever the gentleman, John,' said Constance appearing at his side, and slapping Pauline hard across the face and then shoving her back on to the pew.

'I told you I can't stand weak women,' she said. 'Well I don't like defiant ones either. Now keep still and quiet or I *will* deliver you to the Chinaman.

Mike groaned as he lay in the aisle and watched his wife, whom he had let down so badly, being beaten by the criminals he'd brought into her life. There was nothing he could do to help but he couldn't just lie there. He dragged himself towards the pew Pauline was sitting on, crying out at the pain it caused him. Constance turned towards him. 'A bit too late to think about coming to the rescue isn't it?' she said. 'And you're hardly a knight in shining armour. Stay exactly where you are, unless you want to feel my heel on that knee of yours.

Mike slumped back on to the floor and began to sob.

'Be quiet you pathetic...' The right word escaped her for the moment, as Mike's mobile phone started to ring. 'I need silence while I speak to the nice policeman. Hello inspector, does my chariot await?'

'The ambulance is as close as we can get it to the door. The keys are in the ignition, and we're all standing back. But you do know I can't just let you drive away?'

'I think you can Inspector. In fact, I don't think you have a choice.'

'Leave Mr and Mrs Derbyshire behind and I'll let you take the ambulance.'

'Don't be silly Inspector. You know I can't do that. The Derbyshires are my only currency in the position in which I find myself. And anyway, Mr Derbyshire really needs to be taken to a hospital. I think I owe him that much, since I am responsible for his injuries. Injuries which will get much worse unless you allow me to leave with my guests unhindered. And of course, you must not follow me.'

'Come off it Constance. You know I need some concession from you before I can let you go. That's how it works.'

'Not with me it doesn't,' said Constance, as she removed her gun from her handbag and pointed it at Mike's other knee. Mike screamed in anticipation of the pain and screwed his eyes tightly closed, still holding his injured knee with both hands. He didn't see Constance point the gun into the air before firing it, but he did feel the agony as she ground her heel through his fingers and into his wounded knee.

DI Barton and his colleagues heard Mike's blood curdling screams and presumed he'd been shot again, just as Constance Tyler wanted. Barton looked at DI Jackson, who shrugged his shoulders and said, 'She's an absolute psycho, Dick. I don't see what else you can do.'

Barton nodded and spoke into his phone, 'OK, you win. You can take the ambulance.'

'And you won't follow us will you Inspector? Otherwise I'll have to start on *Mrs* Derbyshire.'

'No, we won't follow you.'

As Constance ended the call, Barton addressed the armed units. 'They're coming out. Keep your weapons trained on them but do not shoot. They have two hostages, one severely injured and they'll make sure they are well covered by them. We can't risk injuring the hostages. Bill, can you get some unmarked cars in place around the area immediately? We need to pick these buggers up as soon as we can. We can't let them simply drive off.'

'I've got a couple nearby already. I'll deploy them and get another couple in. I'll get a chopper in the air as well. They won't lose us.'

'Good. Now everyone, stay calm *and* focussed. That door will open in a minute and I don't want any accidents.

The armed officers adjusted their stances, making sure they were well set and their weapons comfortable and steady against their shoulders. They were used to aiming at human targets and hoping they wouldn't have to fire, but this was different. The targets were going to drive away scot free, and one man was not prepared to let this happen. As Wayne Whitehead watched the church door, sweat trickled down his temples and his eyes narrowed. This was the reason he'd joined the force in the first place, to bring down scumbags like this. Scumbags like the ones who'd encouraged his father to run up crippling gambling debts and then put the screws on him, dragging him deeper and deeper until he'd lost everything he'd ever worked for; his savings, his house – his family's home – his self-respect. When everything was gone Wayne's father had overdosed and died in a back alley in the city centre, leaving Wayne's mother and three children with nothing. Wayne had been thirteen years old then. Old enough to understand but not old enough to do anything other than try to help his mother bring up his younger brother and sister. As soon as he was old enough, he'd joined the Police, still driven by his need for revenge. Today was another step on his road of retribution. This may not be the same people as those who destroyed his father, but they were in the same business and they were going nowhere today – nowhere except to Hell. He was going to prevent their escape – whatever the cost to him... or the hostages.

PC Whitehead watched as the church doors began to open. A woman appeared, head down, her long, light brown hair hanging down totally obscuring her face. There was a gun against her head, held by another woman with short bright red hair – his first target. Wayne could see the heads of two men behind the two women but he focussed his aim on the woman with the short red hair. He reset himself, the air was completely still, no wind to account for, and took careful aim.

CHAPTER 21

Alibi/Road Race/YMCA

Constance Tyler had her left arm tightly around Pauline Derbyshire's neck, whilst her right hand held a gun against her hostage's temple, as they stood together momentarily between the open church doors. Constance could see a couple of Police cars about a hundred yards away and thought she could see rifles trained on her, resting on the car bonnets and roofs. The ambulance was parked immediately in front of her, with the driver's door and the back doors open exactly as she had ordered. This might just work after all. The Police knew who she was and what she'd done. There was no alibi; no way out for her and John through the courts, that was certain, but an escape from Leeds and then from the country might just be possible. There really was nothing the Police could do. The clouds formed an unbroken pale grey blanket over the perfectly still air, as though the world were holding its breath for her next move. This was her moment. 'Come on Pauline,' she said. 'Let's get you

182

into the ambulance.' She gave Pauline a gentle shove and they took a step forward, unaware that PC Wayne Whitehead was holding his breath as his finger tightened on the trigger of the rifle aimed at Constance's head.

As Whitehead's finger squeezed the trigger, a sudden gust of wind hurled the church doors against the two women, knocking them to the floor. Constance's gun was knocked from her grasp and out of her reach, and the bullet from the PC's rifle thudded into one of the thick wooden doors.

From around the corners of both sides of the church half-a-dozen uniformed and plain clothes officers, led by DI Barton, emerged and rushed to the still open church doors. Barton picked up Constance's gun and aimed it at her.

'Good afternoon Ms Tyler. Nice to put a face to the voice.'

Barton heard a voice roar and became aware of a shape moving rapidly towards him through the church doors. The figure was moving far too quickly for Barton to react, but just as John Kilgallon was about to launch himself at the inspector a shot rang out, and Kilgallon was thrown backwards off his feet.

In a matter of seconds the armed response officers had taken control of the situation, and Constance Tyler and John Kilgallon were on the ground with half a dozen rifles trained on them. One paramedic was checking Kilgallon's shoulder wound while another was in the church tending to Mike Derbyshire. Within minutes another ambulance had arrived, and Mike and Pauline Derbyshire were being taken to hospital in one, while John Kilgallon, with an armed escort, was taken away in the other.

Constance Tyler said not a word, but there was fire in her eyes as she was handcuffed and placed in the back of a Police car.

'Right Dick,' said DI Jackson. 'My lads will tidy up here. We'll do the preliminary interview at my place, OK?' he nodded towards Constance.

'OK, Bill. I'll meet you there,' replied Barton. 'I need to get Lisa sorted first. She's still over there with your PC.' Jackson nodded his agreement and got into the passenger seat of the car holding Constance, and was driven away.

'Right Ashworth, put that in the boot,' said Barton, indicating the holdall full of money his DC was holding. 'You can book that in at Scarborough when you get back. Let's go and see Lisa. We'd be nowhere without her help - can't leave her hanging about.'

As he drove across the wasteland with DI Barton at his side and DC Pullman in the back of the car, Ashworth half-turned to his senior officer. 'Sir?' he said.

'Yes, Constable?'

'What exactly happened back there?'

'What do you mean?'

'Well, somebody took a shot without being ordered and someone would have been killed if the doors hadn't suddenly been blown closed.'

'Yes, DI Jackson and I will be looking into that.'

DC Ashworth looked pensive, opened his mouth as if to say something, but closed it again.

'Spit it out Ashworth. There's something else bothering you.'

'Oh, you'll just say I'm being stupid.'

'Well that's never stopped you before has it? Come on out with it.'

'Well, it's just... if the wind hadn't blown the doors closed, that shot would have hit Tyler and maybe Mrs Derbyshire.'

'That's true. So?'

'So where did the wind come from? It was totally still before and after. I remember thinking that the armed response guys didn't have to worry about the wind and yet it absolutely slammed the doors into Tyler... and then it was gone again.'

Barton smiled. 'We just got lucky Ashworth. Saved us a chase round Leeds and potentially a very messy ending. Or are you suggesting some sort of divine intervention?'

'No, sir: not me.' DC Ashworth replied, unconvincingly.

'Look, Martin,' said Barton. 'I know it all started with a phoney vicar falling down the stairs in his church, just before he was going to abscond with the church funds. And it's ended in another church with the church door slamming on to our villains. But let's just take that for what it is OK? A coincidence.'

'I thought you didn't believe in coincidences, sir.' said the DC as he pulled to a stop next to Lisa and her young protector.

'Well I do in this one,' said Barton. 'Let's leave it to the local press to make the divine connection. We'll just write up our reports.' Then he got out of the car and spoke to the young PC standing next to Lisa. 'You'll be taking me back to your station in a minute Constable. You can wait in the car.'

'Yes sir,' replied the PC.

'You OK Lisa? How much could you see from back here?' asked Barton.

'Not much she replied. 'We heard a couple of shots and saw the ambulances. I wanted to come and see what was going on, but *he* wouldn't let me.'

'Good for him,' said Barton, smiling. 'Well, Mike's been injured – shot in the leg actually but don't worry he'll be all right. He's been taken to hospital with his wife.'

'His wife?'

"Yes, she was slapped around a bit. She's just gone for a check-up. Do you want us to take you there to see Mike?'

'Well, I'm not sure – if his wife's there. And to be honest I could do with going home first.

I need to ring work, freshen up, and just well... wind down or something. I feel a bit weird.'

'That'll be shock. You're not used to seeing a shoot-out,' said DC Ashworth.

'And *you are,* I suppose?" said the Inspector. 'And it wasn't a shoot-out, as you put it. OK, Lisa. We'll need a statement from you, but DC Ashworth can take you back to Scarborough and do that there. Then you can get off. He'll let you know which hospital and ward Mike's on and then you can go and see him whenever you're ready.'

'Thank you Inspector.'

'It's me that should be thanking you Lisa. Without your help who knows what would have happened to the Derbyshires? Ashworth, look after her and drive carefully. You're not in a road race to get back – even if DC Pullman does want to get back in time to take his wife to the theatre.'

'Yes sir,' replied the DC. 'Looks like someone's getting a rollocking.'

DI Barton followed Ashworth's gaze to the armed response unit standing nearby. The officer in charge did seem to be tearing a strip off one of his men: no doubt the one who'd fired the first shot. Was he the one who'd fired the second shot, wondered Barton – the one that had possibly saved his life? 'As I said, there'll be a thorough investigation of what happened.'

Lisa looked intrigued, and DC Ashworth said, 'Come on Lisa, let's get going; I'll tell you all about it in the car. You can drive, if you like Pullman. I'll sit in the back with Lisa.' DC Pullman took the keys and DI Barton watched as they pulled away, giving Lisa a friendly wave.

An hour and a half later DC Ashworth was carrying the holdall, containing over nineteen thousand pounds, into an interview room at Scarborough Police Station. Lisa walked alongside him carrying her own holdall. DC Pullman had already taken his leave and headed off home. They placed the holdalls on the table in the centre of the small bare-walled room.

'Would you like a coffee?' asked Ashworth. 'Then we'll get your statement down and you can get off to see Mr Derbyshire.'

'Thank you,' she said. 'But I'm not sure I really want to go and see him. I'm really not that close to Mike. We only met last night. We talked and I felt sorry for him. To be honest I think he's a complete loser. I just felt I should do something to help him today. He was obviously totally out of his depth.'

'Really?' said DC Ashworth. 'You mean you and him are not...together?'

'Of course not,' replied Lisa. 'I prefer my men to be on the *right* side of the law. Always had a bit of a thing for policemen actually.'

'Honest?'

'Oh yeah! In fact...'

'What?' asked the young DC leaning forward.

'Oh, nothing. I don't suppose you're allowed...'

'Allowed what?'

'To go out with a witness. As a policeman I mean – like Doctors can't go out with their patients.'

DC Ashworth was blushing, 'No, there's no rule like that for policemen and witnesses,' he said. 'At least not that I've heard of.'

'But you'll have, what was it DI Barton calls them? A bus conductress?'

''Yes. I mean no. I mean yes, that's what he calls them but no, I don't have one – a girlfriend at the moment.'

'You don't?' smiled Lisa.

There was an awkward silence that seemed to last forever before Lisa said. 'I could murder that cup of coffee now.'

'What? Oh! Yes! sorry! I... Milk? Sugar?'

'Just milk,' Lisa grinned.

DC Ashworth leapt to his feet and left the room almost at a jog. He took the stairs two at a time. He hadn't been this excited about a girl since he'd had his first kiss at a YMCA disco over ten years ago.

The detective constable was back in the interview room five minutes later, having spilled half of the contents of the mugs of coffee in his haste. He saw immediately that Lisa was missing. He stomach churned. She couldn't have! But there was a holdall on the table. No she hadn't. He put the two mugs of coffee on the desk and saw a note.

'Just nipped out for a wee'

Ashworth smiled and sat down and took a sip of his coffee staring at the holdall in front of him. He looked under the table. There was no holdall. Why had Lisa taken hers to the toilet with her? Perhaps there were toiletries in it that she needed. Women were strange creatures when it came to going to the toilet, usually going in pairs and coming back in freshly applied make-up. He'd learned that much in his relatively few dealings with them. He continued to stare at the holdall in front of him. It had pink edging. Did Mike Derbyshire's have pink edging? Surely not. He'd have noticed. He jumped to his feet and pulled back the zip. The bag was full of clothes – a woman's clothes.

*   *   *

Diane Suggett sat in her BMW Mini, a holdall on the seat beside her. A weekend in Scarborough, looking for a bit of fun and an opportunity for a con or two, had turned into a hell of a couple of days.

First she'd hooked up with a bloke who'd just been dumped by his girlfriend (Lisa somebody or other) and ended up smacking him with a bottle, when he found her going through his wallet. Then she'd met Mike Derbyshire and discovered he had nearly twenty grand with him: but despite spending the night with him, she'd been unable to relieve him of it before he'd had to dash off. Of course the most outrageous risk she'd

190

taken had been to go to the Police. But they'd lapped up her story, eager for the inside track her phone calls from Mike had given them. Going back and stealing the real Lisa's holdall had been another risk, but it had turned out to be a stroke of genius. She'd intended to swap it with Mike's after the night they spent together. Instead she'd had to wait until she was left alone in the Police station. The note about going to the loo had just been to gain an extra minute or so. She'd been seen carrying a holdall into the station and so no one questioned her carrying one out.

Poor DC Ashworth. She could just picture his face when he finally opened the holdall on the table. She laughed out loud. Would DC Ashworth see this as more 'divine intervention'? And how was he going to tell DI Barton? 'Dick' was the right name for him. Perhaps *he'd* end up on traffic duty as well.

She started the engine and pulled away, unaware that as she turned the corner, she would be dazzled by the low sunlight as it broke through the clouds, blinding her to the huge sink hole, caused by a collapsed sewer, which was opening up in the road at that very moment. A hole into which her car would plunge.

She chuckled again at the thought of Ashworth and his 'divine intervention'.

The End